CENTRE STAGE

Linda Chapman lives in Leicestershire with her family and two Bernese mountain dogs. She used to be a stage manager in the theatre. When she is not writing she spends her time horse riding, putting on plays and teaching drama.

Books by Linda Chapman

BRIGHT LIGHTS
CENTRE STAGE
MY SECRET UNICORN SERIES

linda chapman

Centre Stage

PUFFIN

PUFFIN BOOKS

Published by the Penguin Group
Penguin Books Ltd, 80 Strand, London WC2R 0RL, England
Penguin Group (USA), Inc., 375 Hudson Street, New York, New York 10014, USA
Penguin Books Australia Ltd, 250 Camberwell Road, Camberwell, Victoria 3124, Australia
Penguin Books Canada Ltd, 10 Alcorn Avenue, Toronto, Ontario, Canada M4V 3B2
Penguin Books India (P) Ltd, 11 Community Centre, Panchsheel Park, New Delhi – 110 017, India
Penguin Group (NZ), cnr Airborne and Rosedale Roads, Albany, Auckland 1310, New Zealand
Penguin Books (South Africa) (Pty) Ltd, 24 Sturdee Avenue, Rosebank 2196, South Africa

Penguin Books Ltd, Registered Offices: 80 Strand, London WC2R 0RL, England

www.penguin.com

First published 2004
1

Copyright © Linda Chapman, 2004
All rights reserved

The moral right of the author has been asserted

Set in Monotype Perpetua
Typeset by Rowland Phototypesetting Ltd, Bury St Edmunds, Suffolk

Made and printed in England by Clays Ltd, St Ives plc

British Library Cataloguing in Publication Data
A CIP catalogue record for this book is available from the British Library

ISBN 0–141–31629–2

To Mrs Carol Davies, my English and Drama teacher, who fostered my love of writing and the theatre when I was at school; and to Keith Loveday, who put up with me spending hours in his office and theatre when I should have been at university lectures, who taught me how to stage manage, build sets, make props and who, most importantly, made me realize that it is always possible to be what you want to be. Thank you!

Chapter One

Never stand on a toilet seat in high-heeled shoes — at least not if you've got an older sister who might bang on the bathroom door at any moment and make you jump. With just five minutes to go before I had to set off for my very first day at Charles Hope comprehensive I was trying to check what I looked like. This meant balancing on the toilet seat to look in the mirror over the bathroom sink.

Of course I *could* have used the full-length mirror in Mum and Dad's room but Dad was getting dressed for work and the idea of seeing him in his underpants was way too embarrassing!

So did I look OK? Bending my knees I checked my top half. White shirt with the top button undone. Navy and maroon school tie pulled slightly down just like Jessica had shown me. Sometimes older sisters can be very useful.

Straightening up I looked at my legs. Navy bootleg trousers, long enough to almost cover my new shoes with their wedge heel. You've no idea how hard I had to beg to get Mum to buy me these shoes. She kept saying I didn't need heels when I was only eleven. But I really do. I'm so small that without heels I look about eight. Luckily, Jess had backed me up and Mum had eventually given in. I looked at my reflection. *Yes*, I thought, feeling pleased. *I look fine.*

Just then there was a loud banging at the door. 'Sophie. Hurry up!' Jess shouted.

I jumped right up in the air and immediately lost my balance.

'Whoaaaa!' I cried as my new heels slipped on the shiny wooden surface. Arms and legs flailing, I crashed to the floor, almost head-butting the bath in the process. Luckily I missed it by about a millimetre. I might not have started secondary school yet but I had a feeling that going in for your first day with a huge red bump on your forehead would *not* have been considered cool.

'Sophie! What are you doing in there?' Jessica said, her voice half alarmed, half irritated.

'Nothing,' I gasped, as I picked myself up off the floor and hastily brushed bits of fluff and dust off my trousers.

'Well, hurry up,' she said through the door. 'I need to brush my teeth and we have to leave in five minutes.'

I hurried to the sink and grabbed Dad's hairbrush that was on the shelf. I dragged it quickly through my dark brown shoulder-length hair. I should have known better. There's something about the hairbrush that Dad uses. My hair just doesn't like it. Immediately flyaway strands floated upwards as if they were magnetically attracted to the ceiling. I tried to smooth it down with my hands but it stood up all the more.

'Sophie!' Jess exclaimed.

'In a minute,' I said frantically. Great, now I was going to go to school looking like a scarecrow. I turned the tap on and splashed some water over my hair. Some of the strands flattened down but others still floated upwards. I groaned. Now I looked like a scarecrow who had been left out in the rain for too long. Why me? Why today?

'I'll get Mum,' Jessica threatened through the door.

'All right, all right,' I exclaimed, opening the door.

'You took your time,' Jessica said sarkily. She did a double take. 'What have you done to your hair?'

'Nothing,' I muttered quickly. It wasn't fair. Jess looked as perfect as always with her black glossy waves caught back in a loose ponytail, a few tendrils framing her oval face, her blue eyes rimmed by smoky-grey eyeliner.

A grin pulled at the corners of her mouth. 'You've been using Dad's hairbrush.'

I gave up any pretence. 'What am I going to do, Jess?' I wailed.

'Put some more water on it and use the blow

dryer,' she advised. 'Here.' She dragged me over to the sink and within seconds had dampened Dad's brush and swept it through my hair. 'There.'

'Thanks,' I said gratefully.

'No problem,' she said pushing me out of the bathroom. 'It's not like I want to be seen at school with a little sister who looks like she's just stuck her hand in an electric socket. Now dry it – quick!'

I ran to my room. For an older sister, Jessica is very cool. Well, most of the time. We hardly ever argue. Not like my best friend, Harriet, and her older sister, Emily. They argue all the time.

I began to dry my hair. I don't usually bother loads about what I wear or how I look. But today was different. Today, my very first day at secondary school, I wanted to look right.

My heart skipped a beat as I thought about what was ahead of me. What if the teachers were horrible? What if I couldn't do the work? What if I got lost? The induction day we'd all been on last term suddenly seemed a very long time ago. I glanced at the framed photo on my desk. So much had happened since last term. The film for a start.

The photo showed me and my friend from filming, Issy, standing with our arms round each other on the set of *A Little Princess*. Being in a film had been the best thing that had ever happened to me. I'd started off by auditioning for a small part but had ended up getting the main part of Sara. It had been brilliant. I'd spent all summer filming. The film was going to be shown in cinemas next year – I couldn't wait to see it.

I looked at Issy's smiling face. She goes to a theatre school in London and she's done loads of films and TV shows. In a few weeks' time, she would be starting acting in a new TV show. Since the film we'd kept in touch by e-mail and I knew she was really looking forward to her new job.

I felt a flicker of jealousy but it quickly faded. After all, it wasn't like there was nothing happening in my life. In just two days' time I was going to an audition for the part of Lucy, in a huge Christmas show of *The Lion, the Witch and the Wardrobe*. If I got the part I'd get to act in a proper theatre every night for two months. I shut my eyes. *I've got to get the part*, I thought, imagining myself standing on a vast stage. *I've just got to.*

'Sophie,' Mum called from downstairs, interrupting my daydream. 'Time to go!'

I turned off the dryer and shook my head. Yes, that looked better. Instead of sticking up, my hair was now hanging straight to my shoulders. Jumping to my feet, I quickly tied my school jersey round my waist and took a deep breath. *OK*, I thought. *Here goes.*

'Sophie!' Ally squealed as I hurried up to the bus stop with Jessica five minutes later. 'I thought you were never coming! Harriet's not here yet either.'

Ally and Harriet are my two best friends. I've known Harriet since we started at playgroup together when we were three, and Ally became our best friend three years ago when her family moved into our village. Ally and Harriet are really different – Harriet's quiet and Ally's definitely not – but we all get on brilliantly.

Leaving me and Ally, Jessica sloped off to talk to her friends.

'I am so glad to see you,' Ally said. 'I thought I was going to be the only one getting the bus.' Considering we were surrounded by about fifteen people all wearing the same maroon-and-navy uniform, it seemed a bit of an odd thing to say. But I knew what she meant. Getting the bus to school with no friends to sit with on the first day would be a total freak-out experience.

'Do I look OK?' Ally asked, her big brown eyes looking at me anxiously.

I checked out what she was wearing. Navy bootleg trousers – the same as mine – tie done in the same way, jersey round her waist, blonde hair curling round her heart-shaped face. 'You look fine,' I told her.

Ally sighed out in relief. She doesn't have an older sister to tell her what to wear. And although her five-year-old twin brothers are cute, if she listened to them she'd be coming to school wearing clothes with Bob the Builder on.

'So, where's Harriet?' I said.

Before she could answer, we both heard a sharp voice. 'Don't you dare come anywhere near me at school, Harriet.'

Ally and I turned. Harriet and her older sister, Emily, were walking towards the bus stop. They look quite similar. They're both tall with freckles and blondey-brown hair. The only difference is that Emily's hair is cut into a bob and Harriet's is long and she always wears it in a ponytail. However, although they look the same, they are very different and they are always arguing.

'Like I'd *want* to hang around with you,' Harriet replied, frowning at Emily. Suddenly she saw us and her face lit up. 'Hi!' she said, hurrying over.

'Hi,' I replied. My heart sank as I looked at her uniform. Harriet is absolutely not into clothes. I'd tried to tell her what to wear so that she would fit in but it was obvious she hadn't been listening. She had tied her tie neatly, she was wearing her school jumper instead of having it around her waist and, worst of all, her trousers were only slightly flared and they finished higher than her ankle, showing off about ten centimetres of sock above her flat, sensible shoes. Definitely *not* a good look.

I wasn't the only one to have noticed. 'What are you wearing, Harriet?' Ally exclaimed.

Harriet looked confused. 'What? It's my school uniform.'

'But your trousers. They're awf—'

'They're a bit short,' I butted in quickly. Ally can be very blunt at times – too blunt.

Harriet looked down at her trousers in surprise. 'No, they're not.' She looked at ours and grinned. 'Just because you two are fashion victims, doesn't mean I have to be too.'

'We're *not* fashion victims,' Ally said.

'No,' I said. It wasn't like we were wearing anything ridiculous; we just wanted to fit in and look like everyone else. I looked at Harriet in confusion. 'I thought I told you what to wear.'

She shrugged. 'You did but I couldn't be bothered looking around for exactly the right sort of trousers and the right sort of shoes. What does it matter anyway?'

Ally and I exchanged looks. What did it matter? I'm sorry but what planet was Harriet on?

'At least loosen your tie,' Ally pleaded.

'OK,' Harriet sighed. 'If it makes you happy.' She loosened her tie slightly and quickly changed the subject. 'So, are you nervous?'

We nodded.

'Me too,' she confessed. 'I couldn't sleep last night. I just know I'm going to get lost.'

'At least we're all in the same form,' Ally put in.

'Yeah,' I agreed. We'd been really worried we were going to be split up into different forms at Charles

Hope but, on the induction day, we had found out that we were all in form 7GD. It was a major relief. Starting secondary school was going to be scary enough; being in a different form from Ally and Harriet would have been dreadful.

'I wish Justine Wilcox wasn't with us though,' Harriet sighed.

Justine Wilcox had been in the same class as us at primary school. We had never got on with her and her friends. All they ever wanted to talk about were boys and clothes.

'Yeah,' Ally agreed. She giggled. 'Do you remember the way she used to hold hands with Kevin in the playground? I mean, how sad was that?'

'She was OK over the summer,' I reminded them. Justine had been an extra in the film and so we had seen quite a bit of each other. On the film set she had been much friendlier than she had ever been at school. 'Maybe she'll be fine this year,' I said optimistically.

'Yeah and pigs might fly,' Ally snorted. 'Justine Wilcox could never be fine.'

'I suppose she might have changed,' Harriet said, trying to be fair as usual.

Just then the bus arrived. We hurried to get seats near the back, not too far from Jess. Tom, my fifteen-year-old brother, sat at the back but he ignored me. He nearly always does when he's with his mates. As I sat down, I noticed quite a few of the people nudging each other and looking at me.

I felt a bit uncomfortable. I knew it was probably because I'd been in the film. There had been articles in several newspapers, including the local newspaper, about how I'd got the part.

A girl with cropped bleached hair who looked like she was about Year Nine came over to me. 'Are you Sophie Tennison?'

'Yes,' I replied.

'My friend says you're some sort of film star. Are you?'

I wasn't sure what to say. If I said yes, that would make me seem like some huge bighead, but I couldn't really say no, either. The whole bus seemed to have stopped talking to listen to me. 'Well, I had the main part in a film,' I said, feeling my cheeks start to go red. Usually I don't mind being the centre of attention but this was weird.

'So you must, like, be really rich, then?' the girl asked. She looked quite tough.

'No,' I said, feeling more uncomfortable than ever.

Jessica stood up. 'She earned some money for the film but most of it's been put in a bank account and she can't use it till she's eighteen,' she said sharply.

The blonde girl frowned at her. 'Who are you?' she challenged.

'Her sister,' Jessica said, eyeing her steadily.

For a moment they both stared at each other. Then, to my relief, the blonde girl seemed to give up on questioning me. With a shrug, she went back to her seat and sat down.

I looked gratefully at Jess. She smiled quickly and then sat back down again with her friend, Nicole.

The conversation on the bus started up again. For a moment neither Ally nor Harriet said anything but then they both spoke at once.

'So, where's Tom today?' Harriet asked.

'What did you do at the weekend?' Ally said.

I smiled at them both. I knew they were trying to stop me feeling embarrassed. I was very glad they — and Jess — were there.

'I am so going to get lost!' Harriet fretted as we headed through the throng of people down a maze of corridors to our formroom. 'I just know I'm going to get lost.'

'Me too,' Ally moaned.

'Jessica told me she once missed a whole Maths lesson because she couldn't find the classroom she was supposed to be in,' I told them.

The noise in the corridor was deafening as everyone all around us discussed their summer holidays. There seemed to be so many people and they all seemed so tall. Bags bumped against me and people pushed past.

'Here we are,' Ally announced as we stopped outside a classroom with a nameplate saying 7GD on the door. GD were the initials of our form tutor, Mr Davey.

As we walked in I felt a rush of relief that the three of us were all in the same form. There were about twenty people in the room already. Some were sitting on their own, others were in small groups. They all looked at us as we entered.

I knew about four other people from primary school. I smiled at them and they smiled back.

'Let's sit there,' Ally said quickly, pointing out three free seats by the window.

We went over. The seats were arranged in pairs. Harriet sat by the window. I dumped my bag on the chair next to hers and Ally sat down at a pair of empty desks just behind us. I looked around.

There was a group of three girls sitting on desks at the back of the room, and near them a large group of boys. On the opposite side of the room to us I could see Saskia Roberts and Julie West, two of Justine Wilcox's friends.

Julie caught my eye. 'Did you hear about Justine?' she called across the room.

'No, what?' I asked, going over to her.

'She's not going to come to school here,' Julie answered.

'Where's she going?' I said in surprise. Justine

hadn't said anything about not coming to Charles Hope when I had last seen her on the film set. In fact, she'd said she'd see me at school.

'She's going to that stage school on the other side of town.'

'What?' I said. 'Clawson Academy of Performing Arts?'

'Yeah, that's the one,' Julie replied. 'She liked being in the film so much that she asked her mum and dad if she could go there and they said yes. She had to have an audition but she got a place and so she's started there now.'

I was stunned. Justine Wilcox was going to a theatre school! She'd get to learn all about acting and be in loads of shows.

'So how come you're not going to a posh stage school, Sophie?' Julie said. 'I mean, with you having been in that film and everything, I'd have thought you'd have gone somewhere like that instead of here,' she said, looking around as if I was mad to want to come to Charles Hope.

I shrugged. I'd never thought about going to school anywhere else apart from Charles Hope. 'I don't know,' I replied. 'I . . .'

A voice interrupted me. 'Hey, are you the girl that was in that film?'

I looked round. It was one of the three girls at the back who had spoken. She had poker-straight shoulder-length brown hair and was wearing mascara and tinted lipgloss. 'Well?' she demanded.

I nodded. 'Yeah, I was in the film.'

Everyone stopped talking – even the boys – and stared at me.

'Cool,' the girl said, glancing at her two friends who were both looking impressed. 'I read about you in the paper.'

I wasn't sure what to say. I settled for smiling in what I hoped was a friendly but not bigheaded way. It seemed to work. The girl jumped off her desk and came over with her friends.

'I'm Kelly,' she said, smiling back. 'This is Leanne,' she nodded to the girl on her left. Leanne had wavy blonde hair caught back in two butterfly clips, and green eyes like a cat's. 'And this is Rachel.' Rachel's sleek black hair was cut into a short bob. 'We were all at Outfields Primary together,' Kelly informed me.

'I was at Ashton Primary,' I told her. I was relieved to see that the boys had lost interest in the conversation and had gone back to their oh-so-mature game of pushing each other to see who would fall off their desk first.

'Why don't you come and sit with us?' Kelly said.

'It's OK. I'm sitting with my friends,' I replied, turning and smiling at Ally and Harriet. Kelly's eyes swept over them but before she could say anything more the door opened and Mr Davey walked in.

He was tall and quite young for a teacher. He'd told us he taught Science and PE. He was followed into the room by a girl with long dark hair and a lady who looked like another teacher.

I quickly hurried to my desk and squeezed in beside Harriet.

'Good morning, class,' Mr Davey said with a smile.

'Good morning, sir,' we all chorused.

'Sit down,' he told us. There was scraping of chairs as we all sat down. The girl and the other teacher stood by Mr Davey's desk. What were they doing there? As far as I could tell every desk in the class was taken.

'Now,' Mr Davey said, looking around at us all. 'It scems we have a slight rearrangement to make.'

What did he mean? I shot a look at Harriet. She looked as confused as me.

'This is Sunita Modi,' Mr Davey said, smiling at the girl beside him. 'She and her twin sister have just enrolled at the school and seeing as their parents wish them to be in different forms, she will be coming to join you lot and her sister will be in 7MF – Mrs French's form,' he said, looking at the teacher. 'However, seeing as this form is full, this means one of you lucky things can escape having me as a form tutor and move across to Mrs French's room.' He looked down at a note stuck to the top of his register. 'And the winner is . . . Alexandra Swannick. Alexandra, would you stand up, please.'

Ally. My heart seemed to stand still. *No, he couldn't mean Ally*. My eyes flew to Ally's face. She had gone as pale as a ghost. She stared at Harriet and me, her eyes wide with alarm.

'Alexandra?' Mr Davey said, looking around.

Shooting Harriet and me a desperate look, Ally slowly got to her feet.

Mr Davey smiled at her. 'Well, your luck's in, Alexandra. Meet Mrs French – your new form tutor.'

'Hello,' Mrs French said warmly. 'Pick up your bag and come with me.'

'But . . . but . . .' Ally started to stammer.

I looked frantically at Harriet. Ally *couldn't* move forms! Harriet looked as frantic as me.

'Yes?' Mrs French said to Ally.

Ally bit her lip and then shook her head and didn't say anything more. But then what could she say? No, I'm not going? Somehow I didn't think that would go down too well.

'Sunita, if you sit where Ally was sitting,' Mr Davey said.

Sunita came down the aisle and Ally had no choice but to leave her desk.

Mrs French smiled at her. 'Your new formroom is just across the corridor.'

Ally threw a last desperate look at Harriet and me, and then Mrs French ushered her out of the door and she was gone.

Chapter Two

'Right, then!' Mr Davey said, clapping his hands together. 'Let's start with the register.'

My mind was in a whirl. I couldn't get my brain round what had just happened. Ally was going to be in a different form. Harriet and I would *never* see her – at least not in lessons.

'What are we going to do, Sophie?' Harriet whispered in dismay as Mr Davey opened the register.

'I don't know,' I whispered back. This was a total nightmare. We'd never been separated – not ever.

'No talking, please,' Mr Davey said.

After Mr Davey had finished the register, he gave us out our homework notebook and we had to write our weekly timetable down in the back.

'Look, we get a double Maths lesson on Monday and Thursday,' Harriet pointed out.

Harriet loves Maths. Actually she loves all subjects. She's mega-brainy. She got to do all the extension papers when we did our SATs last term. Seeing Harriet's eyes positively shining at the idea of double Maths, I suddenly missed Ally. 'Great,' I sighed.

'You never know,' Harriet said optimistically. 'You might start liking Maths here.'

'Yeah, right.' There was about as much chance of me liking Maths as there was of me demanding maggots for breakfast every day.

The bell rang.

'OK – class dismissed,' Mr Davey said as we all began to put our homework books away in our bags. 'Your first lesson is Maths. Go out of here and turn left. The Maths block is just across the courtyard.'

Harriet jumped eagerly to her feet. 'Come on.'

I followed her slowly.

It was strange having to walk to a different class-room for our first lesson. In primary school we'd stayed in one room most of the day with the same teacher, but now we had to take all our books with us and go to see a different teacher for each lesson. I was sure if I didn't get lost I was going to forget the books I needed.

'Where shall we sit?' Harriet said when we reached the Maths room.

'Not too near the front,' I replied. I hate being right under the teacher's nose.

'All right, but not too near the back either,' Harriet compromised. 'We want to be able to see the board clearly.'

'Sophie!'

Hearing my name called out, I looked round. It was Kelly who had spoken. 'Do you want to come and sit by us?' she said, nodding to a spare desk next to Rachel at the back of the room. It was the only desk left in the back row.

'It's OK, thanks,' I told her. 'I'm going to sit with Harriet.'

'Let's go over here, Sophie,' Harriet said, heading for two desks in the third row.

I smiled quickly at Kelly and followed Harriet.

As I sat down I heard a suppressed snigger from the back of the room. I glanced round. Rachel and Leanne were leaning close to Kelly. All three of them were looking at the gap between Harriet's trousers and her shoes. Kelly was whispering something and the other two were grinning.

My cheeks flushed. OK, they weren't laughing at me but I felt embarrassed for Harriet. I turned away quickly.

'I wonder what our teacher will be like?' Harriet said enthusiastically as she got her books out. 'I hope we don't get Mr Jenson. Emily had him in Year Eight and she was always going on about how strict he is.' She began to line up two pencils, a rubber and a ruler very neatly on her desk.

Just then the door opened and our teacher came in. It wasn't Mr Jenson; it was an oldish woman called Miss Foster. 'We're going to start by looking at types of numbers,' she said as we all settled down. 'Who can tell me what a squared number is?'

Harriet and a few of the others put their hands up.

'Yes?' Miss Foster said to Harriet.

'A squared number is a number multiplied by itself,' Harriet said promptly.

'Good. And who can tell me what a cubed number is?'

A boy at the back answered that question.

'And what about the square root of a number?'

Harriet's arm shot out. She was the only person to put her hand up this time.

Miss Foster smiled. 'Yes?'

The words rushed out of Harriet. 'The square root of a number is the number you start with when you square a number, so the square root of twenty-five is five and the square root of a hundred is ten. You can only find the square root of a positive number and every real number has two square roots.'

'Very good,' Miss Foster said, looking impressed. She checked her register. 'Harriet Chase, isn't it?'

Harriet beamed. 'Yes, miss.'

'You got a level six on your SATs, didn't you?'

'Yes, miss.'

'Very impressive.'

Around us I could feel a few people exchanging looks, and from the back I heard an unmistakable snigger. I swung round. Kelly was rolling her eyes mockingly at Leanne and Rachel. I quickly turned back to the front. Harriet grinned at me. I could tell she was really pleased at being noticed by Miss Foster. I forced myself to smile back but inside my tummy felt like it had a hyperactive goldfish squirming round inside it. Something told me that Harriet's keenness wasn't going to go down very well at Charles Hope.

The rest of the lesson passed in a haze of boredom. *Square numbers, prime numbers, factors, multiples . . .*

The words spun round meaninglessly in my head and when we were told to start an exercise in our Maths books, my thoughts drifted to the audition at the weekend. What was it going to be like? I chewed on my pencil. I had prepared a speech to do – it was the start of one of the scenes in the film. Excitement shivered through me as I imagined standing on the big stage at the theatre, looking out at rows and rows of seats and saying my lines . . .

The clack of Miss Foster's heels jerked me out of my daydream. I quickly bent my head over my work and wrote down a number – any number – just so it looked like I was working. School can be so boring at times.

'Sophie! Harriet!' As we made our way along the crowded corridor that led out of the Maths block we heard a familiar voice behind us.

'Ally!' I exclaimed, swinging round.

21

Ally pushed her way towards us. 'I thought you were never going to stop. I've been calling to you from right the way down the corridor.'

'How are you?' Harriet asked.

'Miserable. It's awful I'm not in the same form as you. I don't like any of the girls in my form.'

Sympathy swept over me. 'It's not fair. Why did they have to pick you?'

'I don't know,' Ally moaned.

'We'll meet up every break and lunch,' Harriet promised.

Ally looked relieved. 'So have you just had Maths too?' she asked as we all headed outside.

'Yes,' Harriet said eagerly. 'It was brilliant. We've got a really good teacher and everything we did was really interesting.'

Ally looked at me. 'And translated into non-maths-genius speak?'

'Boring,' I grinned.

Ally grinned back and I felt a rush of happiness. It was so nice being the three of us again. We sat down on a low wall that bordered a grassy bank. It was sunny and it felt good to be outside instead of stuck in a stuffy classroom.

'So, didn't you like anyone in your class?' I said to Ally.

She shrugged. 'A couple of the girls seem OK I suppose.' Her eyes suddenly sparkled and she leant forwards. 'And some of the boys are quite nice,' she said, dropping her voice. 'There's this one called Nathan. He sat near me in Maths. He's got brown hair and it's sort of spiky.'

'You fancy him!' I squealed.

'Well, he *is* cute.' Ally grinned. 'So, what about the boys in your class?'

I thought back. I hadn't really taken that much notice. 'I guess there are one or two who are OK,' I replied.

Harriet nodded. 'There was that one by the door in Maths – Jake, I think he's called. He's quite fit.'

Ally giggled. 'I wonder who's going to be the first of us to get a boyfriend?'

We all exchanged hopeful grins. None of us had ever been out with a boy – not properly. All we'd ever done was hold hands with boys a few times. However, in secondary school things were going to be different. There were loads more boys for a start.

'Whoever gets a boyfriend first has got to tell the others all about it. Agreed?' Ally said.

'Agreed!' Harriet and I replied together.

'Particularly if they kiss,' Ally added.

'Definitely,' I said.

'One hundred per cent definitely,' Harriet said.

'One hundred and fifty per cent definitely!' Ally declared.

'Actually you can't really have one hundred and

fifty per cent, Ally,' Harriet corrected her. 'You see one hundred per cent is actually the maximum that . . .'

Ally and I glanced at each other and then at precisely the same moment began to tickle Harriet in the ribs.

'No!' she squealed, gasping with laughter and falling back on the grassy bank. 'Get off! Get off!'

I grinned as we released her. It was brilliant to be back together.

The day flew by in a blur of lessons. History, French, English . . . By three o'clock it was a relief to collapse on to the bus.

'I can't believe they gave us homework on our first day,' I complained as my bag, full of new books, hit the floor of the bus with a dull thunk. 'I mean, how unfair is that?'

'I know,' Ally agreed.

Harriet opened her homework notebook. 'We didn't get *that* much. Finish the exercise in Maths, write a page about our life and our family for English and read a chapter of our History book.'

'And answer the questions at the end of the chapter,' I groaned. 'It's tons!'

'You think you've got it bad, Soph,' Jessica said, turning round in the seat in front. 'Wait till you're in Year Ten.' She looked at Dan, her boyfriend, who was coming back to ours for tea. 'It's a nightmare, isn't it?'

Dan nodded. 'Every single teacher we've had all day has started the lesson by giving us a lecture on how we've really got to start working hard and thinking about the exams this year,' he told us. 'I don't think they expect us to have a life!'

Jessica sighed. 'I wish I was back in Year Seven.'

'Me too,' Dan agreed.

I couldn't imagine Dan in Year Seven. He's really good-looking, sort of like Freddie Prinze Junior, with short dark hair and a really nice smile. For a while in the summer he and Jessica had broken up but now they were back together and they seemed really happy. I wished I could find a boyfriend like Dan.

I looked hopefully round the bus. A group of Year Seven boys were sitting at the back. They seemed to be having a burping competition. Gross!

Near to them, my brother Tom was sitting with his mates, their feet propped up on the seats in front. They weren't much better. A year ago they had all been fairly normal but then they'd started a band called the Blue Lemons and now they were all growing their hair. They looked totally weird.

What's the matter with boys? I thought. *Why are there so few normal ones?*

When the bus stopped we all piled off. Ally and Harriet had arranged to come back to mine.

'Are you coming home, Tom?' Jess called as Tom slouched off the bus.

'Nah. Going to Raj's,' Tom replied.

Harriet giggled as we headed for my house with Jess and Dan. 'Doesn't Tom's hair look funny?'

'Just a bit!' I grinned. It was about level with his nose and thick and bushy. He had to keep pushing it back all the time.

'I think it looks quite cool,' Ally said.

'It's got waves like a girl's,' I said.

'Tom's such a poser,' Jess said, shaking her head. 'Him and all his mates.' She smiled soppily at Dan. 'I'm so glad you're not like that.'

I saw Dan's hand tighten slightly on Jessica's. The reason they'd broken up over the summer was that Jessica had kissed the lead singer in Tom's band. For a while she'd got really into the heavy, nu-metal type of music that they played, but now she was back with Dan and back to listening to r'n'b and pop again.

We reached our cottage. It's down a small, quiet street behind the church. There's a front door but no one ever uses it. We always go in through the wooden gate at the side of the house. As soon as we opened the gate, Baxter and Wilson, our two Labradors, bounded out of the back door and down the paved yard.

'Hey, boys,' I said as they greeted us, their tails thwacking into our legs, their tongues licking our hands.

There was a yapping sound and a little West Highland White terrier came racing down from the garden.

'Is this a dog your mum's looking after?' Ally said, bending down to ruffle his head.

I nodded. In the summer my mum had started a pet-sitting business called *Purr-fect for Pets*. It was going really well and she had lots of animals to look after. 'He's called Snowy and he's really friendly. He's staying with us for two weeks.'

'Hi there,' Mum said, coming to the back door. 'How was your first day, then?'

'OK,' I called, fighting my way past the dogs and into the kitchen. 'But Ally's not in the same form as us.'

'Oh no,' Mum said, looking concerned. 'How did that happen? I thought you were all going to be together.'

'We were but then things were rearranged,' Ally replied gloomily. Jessica and Dan headed into the playroom to watch the TV while Ally, Harriet and I all sat down and Ally told Mum the story.

'It's not fair,' she said while Mum got out apple juice for all of us from the fridge. 'It's horrid being in a different form from Sophie and Harriet.'

'It must be,' Mum sympathized. 'But I'm sure you'll make new friends quickly.'

Ally didn't look convinced.

'You will,' Mum told her. 'And look on the bright side, then you'll have your new friends in your form and you'll still be friends with Sophie and Harriet.'

'I guess,' Ally sighed. She looked at me and Harriet. 'But you're not to go off together just because you're in a different form to me.' She sounded as if she was teasing but I saw the worried look in her eyes.

Harriet seemed to see it too. 'Of course we won't,' she put in quickly. 'We'll always be your friends, Ally.'

'Always and for ever!' I said. 'We're best friends and being in different forms isn't going to change that.'

Ally smiled. 'Thanks.'

Mum fetched some biscuits and we stood up to go through to the lounge. 'Hang on, Sophie,' Mum said quickly. 'Before I forget, you need to get your jazz shoes out tonight and see if they still fit. You'll need them for the audition on Saturday.'

'Has the play got dancing in it, then?' Ally asked me.

'Yeah.' My tummy flipped as if I had just gone too fast over a hill in a car. I really wasn't looking forward to the dancing audition. I mean, I can dance a bit but I'm not brilliant. When I was seven I started going to dance lessons in our village hall. I did the classes for three years but then I started getting bored and gave up six months ago. I was a bit worried in case the dance steps at the audition were really hard. 'I hope the dancing at the audition isn't too difficult.'

'I'm sure it won't be,' Mum reassured me. 'Sheila Blake, the casting director, knows how much dancing you've done and she wouldn't have asked you to the audition if she felt that you wouldn't be able to cope.'

I felt a bit happier. Mum was right. Surely this dancing audition couldn't be that hard – could it?

Chapter Three

'OK, everyone, settle down!' Mr Davey clapped his hands together as he came into the classroom the next morning.

Ally hastily jumped off my desk. 'See you at break!' she said to Harriet and me. Grabbing her bag, she slipped out of the classroom before Mr Davey could shut the door.

When Mr Davey had finished taking the register, he told us about a noticeboard where you could sign up to join all kinds of different school clubs. 'There are clubs to suit everyone,' he told us. 'Art club, the computer club, quiz club . . .'

'I'd like to join the quiz club,' Harriet whispered to me. 'Can we go to the noticeboard at breaktime?'

I nodded.

Mr Davey told us some more about the different clubs and then we moved on to the day's form activity. Each day our form had a different theme for the day. On Fridays, the theme was going to be reading.

'Next week I'd like you all to bring along a book you are reading,' Mr Davey explained. 'But for today,

I thought we'd start with a discussion of your favourite books.' He walked round to the whiteboard. 'Now, who's going to start us off?'

Harriet's arm shot up into the air.

'Harriet?' Mr Davey said, smiling at her. 'Tell me your favourite book or author.'

'I like loads of books,' Harriet answered. 'All the C. S. Lewis books and the Harry Potter ones; and then there's Philip Pullman, I really like his books, and William Nicholson.'

Mr Davey could hardly write fast enough to keep up with her. 'Well, that's certainly given us a few to start off with. You obviously read a lot, Harriet.'

'I love books!' Harriet replied enthusiastically

I heard a muffled giggle from behind me. I swung round. Kelly was rolling her eyes at Leanne and Rachel. They sniggered.

'Settle down at the back,' Mr Davey said, looking sharply at them.

'Wasn't that interesting?' Harriet said, her face glowing happily as we all picked up our bags to go to Geography after the bell had rung. 'It was really cool to talk about books like that.'

'Very cool!' Kelly said sarcastically as she walked past. 'If you're teacher's pet.'

At her side, Rachel and Leanne grinned.

I saw the happiness fade from Harriet's face. 'What?'

Kelly, Rachel and Leanne walked off giggling together.

'Swot,' I heard Kelly say in an undertone.

I glared after them. 'Idiots!' I said witheringly. I looked across at Harriet, expecting her to shrug off the comments and nod in agreement. But to my surprise she was looking upset.

'What did they mean?' she protested. 'I wasn't being a teacher's pet. I was just answering the questions Mr Davey asked. It was really interesting.'

I felt taken aback. Harriet might be quiet but she's never been bothered about what people say about her. At primary school people used to tease her for being brainy but she always just laughed it off. 'Forget it,' I advised. 'They're not worth stressing about.'

Harriet nodded slowly but she still looked unhappy.

'Come on,' I told her. 'Let's go to Geography.'

'Art club, that sounds cool!' Ally exclaimed as we stood on tiptoe and peered over people's shoulders at breaktime. Apparently we weren't the only ones who'd decided to come and take a look at the clubs' noticeboard.

'Can you see anything about a drama club?' I asked as Ally wormed her way to the front of the crowd. There was a tall boy in front of me who was signing up for the computer club and his head was blocking my view.

'Yeah, there's a notice here. It says that they meet on Friday lunchtimes,' Ally told me. 'They're doing a production of *Grease* at the end of term but you have to be free to rehearse in the evenings.'

'Oh,' I said. I wondered whether to sign up. I wanted to but if I got the part in *The Lion, the Witch and the Wardrobe*, I would be too busy to rehearse. I decided to wait until after the weekend.

'I'm going to sign up for the art club. It meets on Monday lunchtimes,' Ally said. 'How about you, Soph?'

I shook my head. I like art but I didn't want to spend a lunchtime doing it.

A girl from Ally's class was writing her name on the art club list. She turned. 'Shall I put your name down, Ally?'

'Thanks, Eve,' Ally said. She looked at Harriet. 'How about you, Harriet? Do you want to do it?'

'No. I'm just going to do the quiz club,' Harriet replied. 'They've got try-outs next week,' she said, pointing out the notice. 'It says if you're good enough you're allowed to join the club, and then at the end of term the best people get picked to go in an inter-school tournament.'

It sounded just Harriet's sort of thing. She signed her name on the notice.

There was a snort. 'Now *there's* a surprise,' Kelly's voice giggled from behind us. '*Not!*'

Harriet and I looked round. Kelly, Leanne and Rachel were smirking in Harriet's direction.

'I might have guessed that'd be what you'd go for, Harriet,' Kelly said.

'What's that supposed to mean?' I demanded.

Kelly looked taken aback. It was clear she hadn't expected me to stand up for Harriet.

'So what if Harriet's signing up for the quiz team?' I went on. I could see Harriet blushing and Ally looking on in total surprise, but Kelly was really beginning to annoy me. 'At least *she's* clever enough!'

Kelly frowned. 'Keep your hair on, Sophie.'

'Excuse me,' a boy behind me said politely. 'Can I get to the board, please?'

As I looked round at him the words I'd been about to say flew out of my mind. He had light brown hair, gorgeous green eyes and an amazing smile. Wow!

'Sure,' I mumbled, feeling myself go red.

'Thanks,' the boy said. The others stared at him. They were all clearly as stunned as I was at seeing a boy with such love-god qualities so close up. We watched wide-eyed as he stepped closer to Harriet. 'Could I borrow your pen, please?' he asked her.

'What? Oh, yes, of course,' Harriet squeaked, two spots of colour jumping into her cheeks as she held out the pen.

The boy took it and signed up his name. Ben Harvey

I read – and then I realized he'd written his name on the quiz-club sheet.

'You're trying out for the quiz club?' Kelly burst out.

The boy looked surprised. 'Yeah. I did it last year too. I was in the under-fourteen team and we won the regional finals. I'm hoping I get to be captain this year.' He looked at her with interest. 'Why? Are you thinking of signing up?'

Kelly hesitated for a nano-second and then nodded her head as hard as if she was one of those nodding dogs in the back of cars. 'Oh yes, we all were, weren't we?' she said, shooting looks at Leanne and Rachel, who quickly nodded too.

The boy smiled. ' Well,' he said, moving out of the way, 'I'd better let you get to the notice, then.'

Kelly, Leanne and Rachel made a dive for the board.

The boy started to walk away and then stopped. 'Your pen,' he said to Harriet. He handed it back. 'Thanks. I'll see you next week at the try-outs, then?'

He made it into a question. Harriet nodded, her hazel eyes wide. 'Yeah,' she said in a half-strangled voice.

The boy smiled and walked away.

Kelly and the others forgotten, Ally, Harriet and I hurried away from the board to a quiet corner by the stationery cupboard.

'Ohmigod!' Ally gasped. 'Was he gorgeous or what?'

'Did you see the way he smiled at you, Harriet!' I exclaimed.

'I bet he fancies you,' Ally said excitedly.

Harriet's face flushed. 'Of course he doesn't. Don't be stupid. Why would he fancy me?'

'Why wouldn't he fancy you?' I said. Harriet's always going on that she's not pretty but it's not true. She's got sparkly hazel eyes with long curly eyelashes and she's tall and slim. Her hair's lovely too – thick and browny-blonde – although she always just wears it pulled back in a ponytail. 'He told you he'd see you next week, didn't he?' I went on. I felt a flicker of jealousy. Why couldn't a boy like that smile at me? I quickly squashed the feeling. It was brilliant for Harriet and if this boy was into things like the quiz club then he'd be just perfect for her.

'I guess he did,' Harriet said. She started to smile. 'Did you see him write his name down? He's called Ben – Ben Harvey.' She sighed. 'It's a really nice name, isn't it?'

'Harriet's in *lurve*!' Ally teased.

Harriet hit her on the arm. 'Am not!' she said, but her face looked all kind of glowy.

'Come on,' I grinned. 'Let's go to the tuck shop.'

We headed to the hall where the sixth formers ran a tuck shop at breaktime. There was a mad scrum round the serving hatch.

'I'll go and queue — or push,' Harriet said, still looking starry-eyed. 'What do you want?'

We handed over our money and told her our orders — cheese Quavers for me and pickled onion Monster Munch for Ally — and Harriet went to join the crush.

Ally and I wandered over to a table to wait. 'Ben was really nice, wasn't he?' I said.

Ally nodded but she was frowning slightly and I had a feeling that there was something on her mind. I was right.

'What was going on with those girls from your class — you know, just before Ben came along?'

'You mean Kelly, Rachel and Leanne?'

Ally nodded.

I shot a look at the tuck queue to make sure Harriet was well out of earshot. 'They've been picking on Harriet,' I said in a low voice. 'I mean not much, just laughing a bit at her trousers and giggling when she answers questions. And, well, they called her a teacher's pet today after registration.'

'Morons.' Ally frowned.

I nodded in agreement. 'Did you see how quickly they signed up for the quiz club when Ben put his name down?'

'Yeah,' Ally said. 'I mean, how obvious was that? They only did it because they fancy him.'

Just then Harriet came back over. We quickly shut

up. Too quickly. 'What are you talking about?' she asked suspiciously.

'Just about . . . about the weekend,' Ally lied. 'Sophie was telling me about her audition. So what time's it on at, Soph?'

'I've got to be there at ten,' I said, trying to make it seem like we'd been talking about it all along. 'It lasts all day. They're going to split us into groups for the acting, singing and dancing auditions. I'm dreading the dancing.'

To my relief Harriet stopped looking suspicious. She smiled. 'I don't know why. I bet you'll get the part. You'll have to ring us and tell us what happened as soon as you get back.'

'I know, why don't I ask if you can both stay over on Saturday night?' Ally said.

'OK,' I agreed. We often have sleepovers at the weekends.

'I'll ask Mum tonight,' Ally promised.

Yap, yap! Yap, yap!

'Not again, Snowy,' I said as, for about the twentieth time, a rubber hamburger was plonked in my lap. 'Aren't you bored yet?'

'He's just a bundle of energy,' Mum said, shaking her head. 'He never seems to stop. Maybe another walk will help tire him out. I've got to drop Tom to band practice but I'll take him out afterwards.'

Just then the door that led to the lounge opened and Tom came in. 'Can we go now, Mum?'

I stared. 'What are you wearing!'

'What?' Tom said, looking down at his clothes. He was wearing a hoody that was about three sizes too big, baggy black trousers with chains strung across them and two belts.

'You look stupid,' I giggled. 'Why do you need *two* belts?'

'It's cool,' Tom answered.

I grinned. 'Yeah. In some sort of parallel universe.'

Tom frowned at me. 'Like you'd know.'

'OK, OK,' Mum said, holding up her hands before an argument could develop. 'Come on, Tom,' she said, getting her car keys.

Tom walked out of the house and down to the gate.

'Now, did you try on your jazz shoes yesterday?' Mum said to me.

I nodded. 'They still fit.'

'Good. Well, make sure you give them a clean before tomorrow morning. Oh and there's an e-mail for you. It's from Issy. See you later.'

As Mum headed after Tom, I went to the computer and switched it on. What was Issy's e-mail about?

It was short but then Issy's e-mails always were.

Hi Soph. Good luck for the audition! I'll be
thinking of you. I start filming in a week's

time. Can't wait! Anyway, e-mail me SOON!
I'm missing you!!!!!!
Love and hugs, Issy xxxxxx

I smiled. It was cool she'd remembered about my
audition. She might not have written much but I was
used to that. Although Issy had promised that we
would stay best friends when filming ended, she never
rang me and her e-mails were always short. I didn't
mind though. After all, I had Harriet and Ally.

I e-mailed a reply.

Hi Issy. Thanks for the e-mail. I'm doing
one of Sara's speeches from the film for the
audition - the one where she's talking to
Melchisedec in the attic. It should be OK
although I'm dreading the dancing audition.
Keep your fingers crossed for me!! Anyway,
how's school? Ally, Harriet and I had a
complete nightmare this week. Ally was moved
to a different form but we're going to all
stay friends. Apart from that, everything's
OK. I'll e-mail you after the auditions. I
better go and clean my jazz shoes now.
Lots of love, Sophie xxx

I sent the message, turned the computer off and went
to fetch the tube of black shoe polish.

My jazz shoes were on my bedroom floor. The toes were scuffed, so I picked them up and began to polish them. As I squeezed on the black shiny liquid, the words from the speech I was going to do at the auditions bubbled up inside my head.

Oh, Melchisedec. It's been a long day – a very long, hard day . . .

Melchisedec is Sara's pet rat. She is talking to him in her attic bedroom. She is feeling cold and exhausted and wishing her father was still alive.

As I ran through the lines, I shut my eyes and imagined saying them on the stage at the Palace Theatre. It would be very different from being on a film set where film crew surround you all the time, even if you're the only actor in the scene. But I was sure it would be OK. When I'm acting I seem to forget where I am. I know it sounds weird but it's as if everything fades away and I become the person I'm pretending to be.

Imagining myself on stage, excitement flickered through me. I couldn't wait . . .

All right, so maybe cleaning shoes with your eyes shut isn't the brainiest thing to do. Amidst the thoughts of the audition, it slowly dawned on me that my hand felt damp. My eyes snapped open. There was black polish all over my fingers. I'd been so lost in my thoughts about the audition that I'd been obliviously spreading shoe polish over my hand. A very cool look – not!

'Great,' I sighed. Dumping the shoes on the floor, I went to the bathroom and began to wash my hands.

But as I scrubbed at my fingers, my thoughts drifted back to the auditions. Just what *were* they going to be like?

✦

Chapter Four

STAGE DOOR. The faded black letters stood out against the dirty-white background of the sign.

'I suppose this must be it,' Mum said.

I looked around. We were standing outside a grey door in an alleyway behind the theatre. 'Are you sure?' I said to Mum. It didn't look anything like the grand gold-painted front entrance of the theatre.

Mum checked the letter in her hand. 'Yes, the instructions say to go to the stage door in Victoria Street. This seems to be it. Come on, let's go in.'

She turned the handle. A man with a beard and a ponytail was sitting behind a glass panel at a desk. He smiled. 'Here for the auditions?'

So we were in the right place, after all.

'It's Sophie Tennison,' Mum said, pointing to the list of names he had in front of him.

The man ticked my name off the list. 'Fine. Just go through that door there and straight to the stage.'

He pressed a button and we walked through a small door and into a high-ceilinged corridor.

I'd never been backstage at a proper theatre before. There were long black curtains hanging from the ceiling and pieces of scenery stacked by the walls. I felt a thrill of excitement.

A woman with short dark hair came over. She was carrying a clipboard and looked super-efficient. 'Hello, I take it you're here for the auditions?' she said briskly. 'I'm Velda Brown, the company manager. Can I take your name, please?'

'Sophie Tennison,' I told her.

Velda scanned down her list. 'Yes, here you are. You're auditioning to play Lucy?'

I nodded.

'Well, good luck,' she told me. 'Now, Mrs Tennison,' she said, turning to Mum, 'the auditions are going to be taking up most of the day. You're very welcome to stay but, if you'd prefer, you can just leave Sophie here and come back later – about three o'clock.'

Mum looked at me.

'I don't mind,' I said. And to my amazement I realized I actually meant it. Being in the theatre felt somehow right. It sounds weird, I know, but I felt like I belonged there.

'Well, if you're sure, I'll go and do some shopping, then,' Mum said. 'I'll come back this afternoon. Good luck!'

She gave me a hug and left.

'We'll be starting very shortly,' Velda informed me. 'Why don't you join the others?'

I walked slowly on to the stage. There were about twenty other people there. A lot of them seemed to know each other and they stood in small groups, talking. None of them took any notice of me.

I looked out into the auditorium. There were rows and rows of empty red seats. Excitement swept through me as I imagined acting on the stage.

'Sophie!' Hearing a familiar voice, I swung round.

'Justine!' I exclaimed.

Justine Wilcox came hurrying towards me. I hadn't seen her for over a month but she looked just the same, with her long blonde hair caught up in two slides and her pale-blue eyes shining.

'Are you auditioning too?' she asked. 'Sheila, the casting director, came in to my new school and did some auditions last week. She invited those of us she was interested in to come along today. She asked me to try out for Lucy.'

Justine was auditioning to be Lucy! I stared at her in shock. Of course I'd known that there would be other people auditioning for Lucy but it had never in a million years crossed my mind that Justine might be one of them.

'So are you auditioning for Lucy too?' Justine asked.

'Yes,' I managed to say. My mind was racing. Justine was good at acting. In fact, when we'd been doing a school play of *The Lion, the Witch and the Wardrobe* she'd ended up getting the part of Lucy instead of me.

'Wouldn't it be cool if we both got to be Lucy?' Justine said.

Had I heard right? 'What do you mean?' I demanded. 'We can't both be Lucy.'

'Of course we can.' Justine looked at me, her blue eyes surprised. 'You do know there's going to be two Lucys, don't you?'

Er . . . no. I shook my head.

Justine seemed to grow a few inches taller. 'In any big show with children, you have two teams of juveniles – that's what child actors are called,' she said importantly. 'One team does one night and the next team does the other night. It's to stop us getting too tired or something.' She smiled. 'I thought *everyone* knew that!'

OK, so now I felt about as big as an ant.

Velda clapped her hands. 'Can you all sit down now!'

As we all plonked ourselves down on the stage, two women and a man joined Velda. One of the women was tiny and slim with very short red hair and a sharp chin. The other woman had shoulder-length grey-blonde hair, wrinkled, tanned skin and huge hazel eyes like a tiger. She spoke first.

'Hello. I'm Claire and I'm the director.' Her voice

was gravelly and sounded like she smoked too many cigarettes. 'This is Dizzy,' Claire said, pointing to the woman with red hair. 'She's the choreographer of the show, and this is Stefan.' She indicated the man. 'He's the musical director.' Stefan and Dizzy smiled round at us.

Claire continued. 'As most of you know, we are looking for two teams of four children to play the lead roles in *The Lion, the Witch and the Wardrobe*. Although there will be singing and dancing involved, we're not looking for perfect technique in singing and dancing. What we want are eight actors who can look like real children on stage. It is your acting skills that I am most interested in.'

Relief ran through me. Acting I could do.

Claire looked round at us with her cat-like eyes. 'The procedure of the day will be like this . . .' She reminded me a bit of Cruella de Vil in *One Hundred and One Dalmatians*. Of course, I don't mean that she looked as if she was about to run off with a carload of cute puppies, but there was something about her that just made you want to look at her.

'You will be split into two groups – boys and girls,' she informed us. 'Girls will be doing acting auditions this morning and singing and dancing auditions in the afternoon. Boys will be doing the opposite.' She smiled. 'Good luck. And try and enjoy your day.'

I joined Velda with the other girls and she took us

down a staircase at the side of the stage and into a large room with pale-green walls.

'This is the green room,' Velda told us. 'You will wait here for your turn to audition.'

I looked around. There were lots of small dressing rooms leading off a big central space, which had comfy chairs and tea- and coffee-making facilities.

'I've got a list of the order in which you'll be auditioning here,' Velda said. 'First of all you're going to come up individually on to the stage to perform the piece you've prepared at home, and then Claire wants to do some group improvisation. At twelve o'clock we'll break for lunch.'

She pinned up the list of names. I was the third name down on the list and Justine was straight after me. 'While you're waiting, feel free to make your-selves a drink.' Velda headed for the door. 'I'll be back in five minutes for the first person on the list.'

She left. I got the speech I was going to do out of my bag. Justine had started to talk to a few of the other girls. I guessed they must be people from her school. But I didn't mind being left on my own. I wanted a chance to go through my speech.

After ten minutes I heard Velda calling my name. I jumped up.

'It's your turn, Sophie,' Velda said.

'Good luck,' Justine smiled as I passed.

I walked out on to the stage, my heart banging like a

drum in my chest. Claire was sitting in the middle of
the auditorium with Sheila, the casting director, and
another couple of people who I didn't know. They all
looked at me and I felt myself beginning to blush. The
stage suddenly seemed much bigger than it had done
earlier.

'When you're ready,' Claire called.

I crouched down on the floor. *OK*, I told myself,
concentrate.

Shutting my eyes, I imagined that I was Sara. I took
a deep breath. The theatre smelt of dust and paint and
people. It was strange but also somehow comforting. I
opened my eyes and looked at the floor. The words
surged up inside me. My nerves vanished. I could do
this.

'Oh, Melchisedec,' I began wistfully, imagining my
pet rat was there in front of me. 'It's been a long day –
a very long, hard day . . .'

As I spoke, the magic I'd felt when I'd been
acting in the film seemed to take over again. Suddenly
I could see the walls of the attic room Sara was in. I
could see the bare wooden floorboards, the tiny hard
bed . . .

At the end of the speech I blinked as the theatre
came flooding back. There was the sound of applause.
I stood up. All the adults in the auditorium were
clapping.

'Thanks, Sophie. That was really great,' Claire

called, standing up. 'Go and take a break and I'll see you for the improvisations and script readings in about an hour.'

I smiled. 'Thank you.'

Waiting for everyone to have their audition seemed to take ages. After Justine had been for her audition she came and sat with me. She seemed pleased with how her audition had gone.

'Just the dancing and singing to do now,' I said. 'I'm not looking forward to the dancing.'

'Really?' Justine said, looking just the tiniest bit pleased. 'I've been going to ballet, tap and modern dance lessons after school at Clawson's since I was four.'

'So what's it like – going to school there properly?' I asked curiously.

'Brilliant,' Justine replied. 'I mean, there's all the normal boring lessons but you get to do loads of acting and dance and music. I love it!'

She told me about the lessons they did – improvisation, character development, lots of singing and dancing, and then we talked about Charles Hope. Justine wanted to know all the gossip about people we'd been to primary school with. We only stopped talking when Velda came into the green room with some scenes from the play for us to prepare.

She put us into pairs. I was with an older girl

called Samantha. She read Susan and I read Lucy.

Samantha was quite bossy but our scene seemed to go well. After all the pairs had been, everyone had to go on stage and Claire split us into two groups. She asked us first to improvise exploring an old house and then to improvise being lost in some woods. It was great fun. It was also interesting watching the other girls who were auditioning for Lucy. They all seemed very good at acting. I wondered which of us would be chosen. *Me,* I prayed. *Please, let it be me.*

When we had all finished, Claire announced that it was lunchtime. 'There's food set out in the green room for you. You will have an hour's break now and then you'll be going with Dizzy and Stefan to do the dancing and singing auditions. OK?'

We all nodded.

'Come on,' Justine said. 'I'm starving!'

I followed her back down to the green room. The acting audition had seemed to go well but would the dancing and singing go as smoothly?

The music from the CD player blasted out. 'OK, guys!' Dizzy called above it. 'One last practice and then I'll watch you. Here we go!' Her voice echoed around the large rehearsal room with its wooden floor. 'Five, six, seven, eight!'

Standing in front of us, she began the dance she had spent the last half hour teaching us.

And spin, step forward and to the side and cut . . . The instructions raced through my head as I tried to keep up with her.

It wasn't too bad. The steps were all quite easy.

Arms out, windmill and hands up . . .

I could do it. A thrill raced through me. I was dancing and doing just fine.

And round and to the side and back and spin . . .

At last the piece of music came to an end and Dizzy pressed the stop button on the CD player. 'Right, two minutes, then I'll watch you. This half of the room first,' she said, indicating my half of the line.

I pushed my hair back from my damp forehead. *I can do this*, I thought determinedly.

'First group!' Dizzy called.

I walked over to the centre of the room with five of the other girls, Justine included.

Standing by the CD player, Dizzy turned the music on and counted us in again. 'Five, six, seven, eight!'

The music blasted out. Concentrating hard but remembering to smile and look as if I was enjoying it, I spun and stepped and twirled. As I finished the final spin I felt a huge rush of relief. I'd done it! OK, I probably hadn't been as perfect as some of the others but at least I hadn't gone majorly wrong.

'Great,' Dizzy said, writing down some notes on a clipboard she was holding. 'Next group into position!'

Ten minutes later the audition was over. As I walked

out of the rehearsal room relief buzzed through me. I'd got through the dancing audition and, miracle of miracles, I hadn't made a fool of myself!

We went to another room with a small canteen in it and waited there while Stefan, the musical director, took us out in groups of four.

The musical auditions were in a small room with a piano. Stefan played a number of scales and we had to sing them and then he taught us the chorus of one of the songs in the show. We had to sing it back to him — first together and then one at a time.

I was in a group with Justine and the two other girls who were auditioning to be Lucy. I think I did OK. Stefan seemed pleased and I only had to sing the chorus once. Justine and one of the other girls had to sing it three times before they got it right.

At the end of the day we all went on to the stage. People were talking excitedly, catching up on how each other's auditions had been. I looked into the auditorium and saw that most people's parents had arrived. Mum was there. Seeing me looking, she waved. I waved back but then Claire walked on to the stage and we all fell silent.

'Well, that's it for today,' Claire said, smiling at us. 'It's been great to see you all. Dizzy, Stefan and I are now going to get together and make some decisions. Thank you all very much for coming. We'll be in touch in the next few days.'

She and Dizzy and Stefan smiled and then walked off.

That was it. It was all over. There was a pause and then everyone started to move. The noise level rose as parents stood up in the auditorium and people began to gather their bags and coats from the wings.

Justine came over to me. 'Well, I'll see you soon, I guess,' she said to me. 'Hopefully at the rehearsals!'

'Fingers crossed!' I smiled.

We said goodbye and I went to meet Mum.

'Well, how was it?' she asked.

'OK, I think,' I replied.

'Well, let's go,' Mum said. 'You can tell me everything you've been doing on the way back home.'

I looked round the theatre. I didn't want to leave. Now I'd spent the day here I wanted the part of Lucy more than ever. I wanted to be on that stage, to act in front of a real audience.

'Sophie?' Mum said.

'Coming,' I sighed reluctantly.

I followed her out of the auditorium. Walking out of the theatre's front doors and on to the busy, bright, Saturday streets, I felt like I had been in another world.

My world, I thought, and I was filled with a sudden desperate longing. I just had to get the part of Lucy — I had to!

Chapter Five

'Now write down four places – two you'd like to go to and two you wouldn't,' Ally instructed, sitting cross-legged on her bed.

I scribbled down Alton Towers, ice skating, school and the North Pole on the four pieces of paper in front of me.

Harriet, Ally and I were sleeping over at Ally's house. Over supper, I'd told Ally and Harriet all about the audition – and Justine, of course. Now we were in Ally's bedroom playing one of those games where you find out who your ideal boyfriend is and what your perfect date would be like. You know the type.

Ally put the pieces of paper in a mug and placed it next to the other mug on her bedside table. That mug had boys' names in – we'd each had to write down two boys we liked and two we didn't.

'So who's going first?' Ally asked eagerly.

'Me,' I said. Ally held out the mugs and I took a piece of paper from each. I placed them in front of me. Then Harriet had a go, then Ally.

'Go on, Soph,' Ally urged. 'Read yours.'

I opened the pieces of paper. Seeing what was written there, I groaned. 'My perfect date would be with Mr Davey and we'd go to the cinema.'

Ally and Harriet burst out laughing.

'Oooo,' Harriet teased. 'Sophie fancies Mr Davey!'

I hit her with a pillow. 'I so do not!'

Still giggling, Harriet opened hers next. 'My perfect date would be . . .' she paused and wrinkled her nose, 'with Tom, Sophie's brother, and we'd go to the North Pole.'

I glanced at Ally. She'd gone slightly red and I knew it was she who had put Tom's name down. I know she fancies him although she'll never admit it. She saw my look and hastily started to open her pieces of paper. 'My turn! My perfect date would be with,' she smiled, 'Nathan and we'd go ice skating. Cool!'

We played three more times and then I suggested we read the problem pages in Ally's collection of *Mizz* and *Sugar* magazines. We all love looking at the problems. Some people ask the most obvious things!

'No, let's read my quiz book,' Harriet said. She reached over and pulled a quiz book out of her bag called *One Thousand Quiz Questions*. 'The quiz club try-outs are on Monday and I've got to practise,' she went on. 'We can all try answering the questions. It'll be fun!' She opened the book. 'Look, here's a question. It's really easy. Who was the first Tudor king?'

Ally looked at me. 'Hmmm, quiz questions or problem pages – it's a difficult choice, isn't it, Soph?'

'Very difficult,' I said, pretending to be serious. 'Now, which would I rather do?'

Ally's eyes met mine.

'Read the problem pages!' we both exclaimed.

'You two,' Harriet said, sighing half in exasperation. But I could tell she hadn't really expected us to say we'd do the quiz questions. 'I guess I'll just have to read it tomorrow. But if I don't do well in the quiz try-outs it'll be all your fault.'

'You *will* do well,' I told her.

'Yeah. And just think, once you're in the quiz club you'll see loads of Ben,' Ally said.

'That's not why I want to get into the quiz club,' Harriet protested. She smiled. 'But it would be good, wouldn't it?'

'I can see it now, him asking you over to his house to practise,' Ally teased. She pretended to be Ben. 'Oh, Harriet, please come to mine and do some quiz questions with me – please,' she said, putting her hands on her heart.

I grinned and sang a song that we used to sing in primary school. 'Harriet and Ben up a tree . . .'

Ally joined in. 'K-I-S-S-I-N-G!'

For a moment Harriet looked annoyed, but as Ally and I made stupid kissing noises, a grin pulled at the corners of her mouth.

'If only,' she sighed longingly.

I woke up early the next morning. As I blinked my eyes open, a prickle of nervousness ran through me. What was I feeling nervous about? Suddenly I remembered the auditions and in an instant, I was wide awake. Of course, I was waiting to hear if I'd got the part of Lucy. When would I know? *Soon, please*, I prayed.

From the regular sound of Ally and Harriet's breathing I could tell they were still asleep. I lay in my sleeping bag thinking about the auditions. They *had* gone well, hadn't they? I hadn't made an idiot of myself in the dancing, and my singing and acting had seemed OK.

A horrible thought crept into my brain. *What if Justine gets to be Lucy and I don't?* She'd been good at the auditions and she'd been Lucy before.

No, it wouldn't happen. I gulped. *Would it?*

Trying to be positive, I shut my eyes and imagined being Lucy. It would be just the coolest thing ever. I'd have to miss school for a start!

At last Harriet and Ally woke up. They were going riding together that day and although I love horses, being around them gives me hay fever, so after breakfast they set off for the stables and I went back home.

'How was your sleepover?' Mum asked. She was in the kitchen, brushing Snowy. From the silence in the house I could tell Tom and Jess were still in bed. But then they almost never get up before eleven if they can help it.

'Good,' I said, dumping my bag on the floor. 'Do you want a hand?' I asked, watching Snowy try to chew the brush.

'Thanks,' Mum said. 'He seems convinced the brush is a toy.' I went over and Mum held him while I gently teased out his wiry white coat with the brush.

'Mum,' I asked. 'When do you think I'll hear about the audition?'

'It shouldn't be too long. All the auditions were held yesterday and they said they'd let people know as soon as possible.'

'So I might find out today?' I said quickly.

Mum nodded. Excitement fizzed through me. I so wanted to know!

'What have you got planned for this morning?' Mum asked.

I shrugged. 'Nothing much.'

'Are you free to come and help me, then?' Mum said. 'I'm looking after the Walters' rabbits again so I could certainly do with a hand.'

The Walters family bred rabbits and had twenty-three of them. Looking after them was a lot of work. 'Of course I'll come,' I said.

Mum smiled. 'Thanks, love.'

*

I helped Mum all morning. As I cleaned out the rabbits' hutches I kept thinking about the play. When would I find out?

I had homework to do in the afternoon, but I couldn't concentrate. I was staring into space and thinking about the auditions when Mum called up the stairs.

'Sophie! Phone!'

Pushing my Maths to one side, I jumped off my bed. 'Who is it?' I said, going to the top of the stairs.

'Sheila Blake,' Mum replied.

My heart did a double flip. 'Sheila!' I gasped.

Mum smiled and nodded. 'Hurry up. Don't keep her waiting.'

Racing down the stairs three at a time, I half fell into the kitchen and grabbed the phone. 'Hello?' I stammered.

'Hello, Sophie. It's Sheila Blake.'

'Hi,' I gasped, barely able to get the word out through my excitement and nerves.

'Well, I've got some good news for you.' I could hear the smile in Sheila's voice. 'You've been given the part of Lucy.'

I gaped like a goldfish.

'Are you pleased?' Sheila asked.

Pleased? I was ecstatic! 'Yes!' I managed to gasp. 'I'm really, really, really pleased!' I looked at Mum. She was grinning at me and I knew Sheila had already told her the news.

I've got the part! I've got the part! The words sung in my head so loudly that I almost missed Sheila's next words.

'Initial rehearsals for the juveniles start on Saturday.' I forced myself to concentrate. 'They'll be held at Clawson Academy of Performing Arts. You'll be needed to rehearse each weekend for the next six weeks and on Tuesday evenings. That won't be a problem, will it?'

'No,' I answered quickly.

'Great. Full-time rehearsals — with the adults in the cast — will start in November, three weeks before the show opens. You'll be taken out of school for those — and obviously for the performances that you're involved in. So we'll need to get you a licence. Do you want to put your mum back on the phone so I can talk about the arrangements in more detail?'

My heart singing with happiness, I handed the phone over to Mum. She took it and began to talk about things like contracts and licences. Ignoring the fact that I probably looked like a hyperactive four-year-old, I jumped up and down on the spot in delight. I'd got the part! I was going to be Lucy!

It didn't take Mum and me long to spread the news. I rang Ally and Harriet and e-mailed Issy, who sent me a message back almost straight away to say congratulations. That evening, Dad bought a huge Chinese takeaway to celebrate. It had absolutely all my favourite things — crispy duck, spring rolls, sweet and sour chicken, beef chow mein. Dad also bought a bottle of champagne.

'This is cool. Do you think you can get a part in a play every week, Sophie?' Tom said, starting to dig into the box and taking out a huge bag of prawn crackers.

'Definitely!' Jess said, helping him.

'I'll get some glasses for the champagne,' Mum said.

Dad peeled the gold foil off the top of the champagne bottle. 'OK, are we all ready?' he said, and he opened the bottle. The cork came out with a loud pop and he quickly poured some champagne into the glasses. He only gave me a little but it was fun to sip at the bubbles fizzing in the pale-gold liquid.

'You did so well, Sophie,' Mum said, hugging me. 'We're all so proud of you. Sheila said you did an excellent audition. Apparently the director was absolutely insistent that you were Lucy.'

'Don't tell her that, Mum, you'll make her even more bigheaded than she already is,' Jessica groaned.

'I suppose this means we've got to put up with you prancing around the house and learning another script,' Tom said teasingly.

'Not only that, but this time you've got to come and see me actually perform,' I told him.

'Oh no,' Tom said. 'Nightmare.' He grinned and

ruffled my hair. 'Just think, isn't it weird? There's going to be loads of people coming to watch you – my bratty little sister.'

'Get off,' I said, shaking his hand away and quickly smoothing down my now standing-upright hair. 'And don't call me bratty!'

But I didn't mind really. It was nice to have Tom teasing me instead of just grunting and ignoring me like he usually did.

'I think it's time for a toast,' Dad announced, holding up his glass. 'To Sophie. For getting the part of Lucy.'

'To Sophie!' everyone said.

I took a gulp of champagne and immediately spluttered as the bubbles fizzed up my nose.

'Very cool, Sophie,' Jessica grinned.

'Yep, very film starry,' Tom teased.

'Shut up!' I told them. But I didn't mind about their teasing. I'd got the part of Lucy. That was all that mattered.

Chapter Six

'It's brilliant!' Harriet said to me for about the hund-
redth time as we walked back to the changing rooms
after PE the next morning. 'Loads of people will come
and see you.'

'I can't wait,' I grinned.

'I wonder if Justine is going to be in it,' Harriet
said.

I nodded. I couldn't believe I hadn't asked Sheila
who the other Lucy was going to be. But I'd been so
excited at finding out that I was going to be Lucy I just
hadn't thought about it.

'I guess I'll find out on Saturday,' I said. 'It's the
first rehearsal then.' Realizing that all we'd done all
lesson – actually, make that all morning – was talk
about me, I changed the subject. 'So, have you been
practising for the quiz?' It was the quiz try-outs that
lunchtime.

'Yeah – are you and Ally going to come and
watch?'

I nodded. 'Course!'

I began to change out of my sports kit – white polo

shirt and maroon shorts — yuk! I'm sure the people who invented our school uniform tried to make it look as disgusting as possible. As I took off my shorts, I glanced surreptitiously round the changing room just to check out what everyone else was wearing. Knowing I would have PE that day, I'd made sure I'd worn high-leg knickers. Jessica had said that it was really uncool to wear anything else. I was also wearing a padded bra with Little Miss Naughty on. OK, so I don't exactly need a bra — in fact, to be honest, I couldn't be further from needing one — but Jessica had told Mum there was no way I could go to secondary school in a crop top or vest, and so when we went shopping for my school uniform, Mum had bought me three bras as well. Looking around and seeing that almost everyone else had a bra on too, I felt very glad.

'I really hope I do well at lunchtime,' Harriet said, taking off her shorts and shirt. 'I want to get into the club so much!'

'Love the pants, Harriet!' Kelly called out.

Harriet looked startled. 'What?' she said, glancing down at her plain white sensible knickers.

'Where did you get them from?' Kelly grinned. 'Some old granny shop?'

'Comfy are they?' Rachel said. 'They're certainly big enough.'

'And the crop top's great,' Leanne joined in.

Harriet went as red as a plum tomato.

'Did Mummy buy it for you?' Kelly said. Leanne and Rachel cracked up.

'Shut up!' I said angrily to them as Harriet turned away and quickly pulled on her school shirt. 'Leave her alone.'

Kelly looked at what I was wearing but seeing as she and I had on almost exactly the same bra and knickers she couldn't find anything to tease me about. Instead she just smirked at the others, and then turned away.

I glanced at Harriet. Her fingers were trembling as she did up her buttons and her eyes were bright with tears. I bit my lip, wondering whether to say anything but I didn't want to, not with Kelly and the others still there.

We got dressed without saying another word. Harriet half ran out of the changing rooms, her head down. Grabbing my bag, I hurried after her.

As soon as we were a safe distance away from Kelly and the others, I looked at Harriet. 'Are . . . are you OK?' I said, feeling awkward.

She nodded, looking at the ground.

'Are you sure?'

'I'm fine,' she replied in an uptight voice.

I hesitated. It was obvious she didn't want to talk about what had just happened. I didn't blame her. I would have been mega-embarrassed if it had been me. Harriet continued to stare at the floor.

'It's French next,' I said, saying the first thing that

came into my mind. 'Have you learnt your verbs for the test?'

Stupid question. After all, when had Harriet ever not done the work for a test?

Harriet nodded but she didn't say anything.

'I hope it's not too difficult,' I babbled, wanting desperately to fill the silence. 'Miss Rogers is really strict. Jessica says she gives out detentions all the time.'

'Yeah, Emily's had a detention from her before,' Harriet said. I saw her shoulders relax slightly and she even glanced at me. 'Emily said if you get less than seven out of ten she makes you do another test the next day and if you don't hand your homework in you get a detention. No warning or anything.'

I felt relieved. Harriet seemed to be recovering. The bell rang. 'Come on,' I told her. 'We'd better not be late.'

'Oof!' I said as Ally nudged me hard in the ribs.

'That's Nathan from my class,' she hissed, nodding towards a boy with brown hair who was walking into the room. 'He's cute, isn't he?'

I nodded.

It was lunchtime and we were in one of the large rooms in the Maths block. A long row of chairs had been lined up by the blackboard for everyone who wanted to be considered for the under-fourteen quiz club. Harriet was sitting there and so were Kelly,

Leanne and Rachel – and Ben. I noticed that Kelly had managed to get the chair beside him.

Ally and I were sitting on desks at the back of the room with the other people who had just come along to support their friends.

'I really think he likes me,' Ally went on, still looking at Nathan. 'He was sitting at the same table as me in art and he kept smiling at me.'

Normally I would have been really interested but right now I had something else on my mind. I wanted to talk to Ally about Harriet being teased after PE. 'Ally . . .'

Just then a girl with dark curly hair and lively hazel eyes stopped beside us. 'Hi, Ally! Can I sit here?'

I recognized her as the girl from Ally's class who had been signing up for the art club at the clubs' noticeboard.

'Sure, Eve,' Ally told her, budging up on the desk.

'So, how come you're here?' Eve asked, squeezing in beside her.

'Sophie and I are watching our friend Harriet,' Ally said, glancing at me. 'Sophie and Harriet are in 7GD.'

'Oh, right,' Eve said, smiling at me. 'Hi. I'm here to watch my friend Sasha. She's in 7NR. That's her, sitting over there,' she said, nodding to a girl at the end of the row. 'She's really brainy. I'd never be clever enough to do something like this.'

'Me neither,' Ally agreed.

'I'd have thought Ruth and Ellie would be here,' Eve said.

'Yeah,' Ally said. 'They're two girls in our class,' she explained to me. 'They're really clever.' She turned back to Eve. 'Nathan's here, though. I wonder if he'll get in.'

'He's really fit, isn't he?' Eve giggled. 'But I think he's quite shy.'

They started talking about Nathan and about some other people in their class. It felt weird listening to Ally talk about people I didn't know. I almost began to feel left out. I looked at Harriet. She was looking nervous but I was sure she was going to be OK. I gave her the thumbs-up sign and she smiled back gratefully.

A few minutes later, a sixth former stood up and clapped his hands for silence. Like most of the clubs, the quiz team was being organized by sixth formers.

'I think we're ready to start,' he announced. 'My name's Andy. I'm the quiz master.' He turned to the people at the front. 'We're going to split you into four teams and ask you questions. Put your hand up if you think you know the answer. If your team gets the answer right you get a bonus question just for your team. It doesn't really matter which team wins; we just want to see how well you react under pressure and, of course, how much you know.'

The quiz started. Harriet answered loads of questions – and got them right. Which was more than Kelly did. She answered about four questions and only got one right. Leanne and Rachel didn't put their hands up at all. Ben was really good. He answered more questions than anyone.

At the end of the quiz, the sixth formers went off into another room to discuss who they would select.

'I bet Harriet's got in,' Ally whispered to me.

I nodded. 'She was brilliant.'

Five minutes later, the sixth formers came back in. 'OK,' Andy said. 'We can now tell you who's been chosen to be in the quiz club.'

I crossed my fingers. Please let him say Harriet's name . . .

'Tania Foggarty, Ben Harvey, Sasha Lawson, Harriet Chase . . .'

Yessssss! I grabbed Ally's arm in excitement. 'She's got in!' I whispered.

'That's your friend, isn't it?' Eve said to Ally.

Ally nodded.

Harriet looked totally delighted. But someone wasn't pleased. Or to be more accurate – three some-ones: Kelly, Leanne and Rachel. None of them had had their names read out. Leanne and Rachel looked as if they didn't really care, but Kelly looked totally fed up.

As soon as the names had been read out I jumped off the desk. 'Come on,' I said to Ally. 'Let's go and see Harriet.'

But as Ally and I hurried across the room, Ben went up to her. We screeched to a stop.

'Look!' I hissed, grabbing Ally's arm.

We were too far away to hear what Ben was saying but Harriet was smiling and talking animatedly. We edged closer. As we got nearer I could hear Harriet saying, 'I so nearly answered that question about the Nile wrong but then I remembered the right answer and . . .'

'Hi, Ben,' Kelly interrupted, walking up to them. 'Congratulations.' She fluttered her mascared eyelashes at him, totally ignoring Harriet. 'You did *really* well.'

Ben smiled. 'Thanks. Sorry you didn't get in, Kelly.'

'Never mind.' Kelly edged round so that her shoulder was almost pushing Harriet out of the way. 'So what else do you like doing apart from the quiz club, Ben?'

'All sorts,' Ben said, stepping back a bit so Harriet was included again. 'I go sailing quite a lot.'

'Really!' Kelly said all wide-eyed. 'I'd *love* to try sailing.'

I'm sorry, but could she be any more obvious? However, to my relief, Ben didn't invite her to go sailing with him. 'Well, um, you should go some time,' he said, looking awkward. 'Anyway, look, I'd better catch up with my mates.' He turned to Harriet. 'I'll see you next week, Harriet.'

Harriet nodded eagerly and Ben disappeared into the crowd.

Kelly stared after him for a moment and then she turned and hurried back to her friends. I forgot about her.

'Congratulations!' I exclaimed, racing over to Harriet with Ally.

'You were brilliant!' Ally cried.

'Thanks,' Harriet said shyly.

'Ben got in too,' Ally said. 'And he likes you!'

Harriet went pink. 'He doesn't,' she said quickly.

'He does!' Ally insisted. 'It was totally obvious when he was talking to you.'

'There's going to be *luuuurve* in the quiz club,' I grinned.

Harriet looked very hopeful. 'I can't wait till the first meeting,' she grinned back.

Although I was really pleased that Harriet had got into the quiz club, the downside was that now Kelly had it in for her even more. She, Rachel and Leanne kept giggling and whispering comments whenever Harriet went by or answered a question in class. I just didn't know what to do. It wasn't like they were really bullying her but I could tell Harriet was getting upset.

I told Ally about it. 'She's just got to ignore them,' she said when I rang her on Friday night. 'If they see she's not bothered then they'll stop.'

'But she *is* bothered,' I told her. 'She hardly answered any questions in Maths today.' I sighed. 'They're just such losers. I mean, if I say anything to them they shut up but then they just start again the next day.'

'Harriet needs to say something to them herself,' Ally said.

'I know,' I replied. 'But she just won't, and she won't even really talk to me about it.'

'Do you think I should try and speak to her about it tomorrow?' Ally asked. 'We're going to be at the stables all day.'

'Good idea,' I said. Maybe away from school, Harriet would talk about it more. I hoped so. It was horrible seeing her getting upset.

'I'll ring you tomorrow,' Ally said. 'Tell you how it goes. Good luck at the rehearsal.'

The rehearsal! My heart pitter-pattered with excitement. 'Thanks,' I said, wondering what it was going to be like. One thing was for sure, I couldn't wait to find out!

Chapter Seven

'Here we are,' Mum said the next day, parking the car outside an old Victorian house. There was a notice-board on its wrought-iron gates which said, *Clawson Academy of Performing Arts.*

I fumbled with my seat belt, my heart turning somersaults.

'So, are you excited?' Mum asked

Excited? I was so excited I could hardly breathe. I nodded. 'Very!'

Mum and I went into the school. There was a signpost with a big arrow which said, *Lion, Witch and Wardrobe rehearsals – Bernhardt Theatre.*

We followed the arrow down a corridor and out into a courtyard. On the opposite side of the court-yard was a modern black-and-white building with the words *Bernhardt Theatre* in big letters over the doors.

'That looks like the place,' Mum said.

We went over to the theatre. Inside there was a small foyer and then double doors which opened into a room about the size of our school hall. There were lots of people milling around. There wasn't a stage but at the side of the room platforms were stacked. The ceiling was high and criss-crossed with metal lighting bars and in the far corner of the room there was a scaffolding tower.

'Hello, it's Sophie Tennison, isn't it?'

Looking round, I recognized Velda. 'Hi,' I said, nodding.

Velda smiled at Mum. 'You can leave Sophie now if you want. She'll be ready to be collected at four.'

Mum looked at me. 'Is that OK?'

I nodded. There were loads of other people my age or a bit older there, and none of them had their parents with them. 'Yeah, I'll see you later, Mum.'

Mum said goodbye and left.

'We'll be starting in about five minutes,' Velda told me. 'Help yourself to a drink and biscuit.' She pointed out a table with big jugs of orange juice on.

I was just about to head over when I heard someone call my name. I looked round. Justine was hurrying towards me.

'Did you get the part of Lucy?' Justine demanded.

I nodded.

'So did I!' Justine beamed.

'Oh, brilliant!' I gasped. 'Well done.' Knowing I was Lucy too, I could feel genuinely pleased for her.

'Were you going to get a drink?' Justine asked.

I nodded.

'Let's go together,' Justine said. We set off towards the drinks table. It was weird how much things had changed since primary school. We had not got on at all then but now, well, now we seemed to be almost friends.

'So, do you like our theatre?' she asked.

I nodded. 'It's cool.'

'The stage is moveable so we can have it wherever we want,' she told me. 'Those doors through there lead to the dressing rooms. Upstairs there's a smaller studio theatre and also the dance studios. I'll show you around later.'

It was strange having Justine know so much and me know so little. As we poured ourselves drinks, I wondered if loads of her friends from school were going to be in the cast. 'Do you know many people who are in the play?' I asked curiously.

She shook her head. 'Not really. From Year Seven there's just me and two other girls. Everyone else is in Years Eight, Nine or Ten, and I only know them by sight.'

Just then someone tapped me on the shoulder. I swung round. A girl who looked about fourteen was standing behind me. She was skinny with dark auburn hair tied in two low bunches. 'Excuse me, but are you Sophie Tennison?'

I nodded.

The girl smiled. 'Velda told me to come over. I'm

Colette Masters. We're in the same team. I'm playing Susan – Lucy's older sister.'

For a moment I hadn't a clue what Colette was going on about but then my brain clicked into gear. Of course. There were going to be two teams of children. I was Lucy in one team and Justine was Lucy in the other.

'Do you want to come and meet the boys who are playing Peter and Edmund in our team?' Colette went on.

'OK,' I said eagerly. I looked at Justine.

'I suppose I should go and meet my team too,' she said. 'See you later, Sophie.'

Colette led me to where two boys were standing. One was tall with blond hair. He looked sporty – like he played rugby or something. The other was smaller with short dark hair and a nice smile. They both looked about the same age as Colette.

'This is Sophie,' Colette announced.

The tall boy turned out to be called Jack; he was playing Peter – the older brother. The other boy was called Mark; he was playing Edmund – the younger brother. He and Colette were at school at Clawson's. Jack was at a private school but he knew them both because they had all been part of the chorus in the Christmas show at the Palace Theatre the year before.

'So you've been in a film, then?' Jack said to me.

'Yeah,' I nodded.

'And you had the lead. That is so cool!' Colette said.

'When's it coming out?' Mark asked.

'Next summer I think,' I replied, feeling a bit awkward. I was proud I'd been in the film but I didn't want them to think I was making out I was some kind of famous film star. 'I haven't done any theatre shows before though.'

'It doesn't matter. It's great that you're in our team,' Colette said. 'It means we're bound to be chosen for the first night.'

The boys nodded.

'First night?' I echoed.

'The director chooses the best team to perform on the first night,' Colette explained. 'It's *the* performance to do. Everyone who's important goes — agents, casting directors, the press. If you're in a big show like this you just have to perform on the first night.'

'It means we've got to really be good in rehearsals,' Mark said. 'You've got to do your absolute best all the time.'

Just then Velda clapped her hands. 'OK, everyone, gather round!'

We all made our way over. Dizzy was standing by Velda. She was wearing a maroon all-in-one footless leotard and a bright-pink ballet top. A purple sweatshirt was tied round her waist.

'Hello, everyone,' she said as the chatter died

down. 'Welcome to the first day of rehearsals. We're going to start with a few introductory games to learn each other's names and then I'll teach you the opening company number. Now, to start off with, let's have you all in a circle.'

For the next fifteen minutes we played games to learn each other's names. First we had to go round the circle saying our name and then we had to throw a ball round saying first our name and then the name of the person you were throwing it to. Then we had to do the same but with an imaginary ball. Dizzy was quite strict. She didn't put up with any giggling or messing around. I had a feeling that you definitely wouldn't want to get on the wrong side of her.

Once we'd got each other's names sorted, we did a warm up. It was fun – a bit like an aerobics class. When we had finished, Dizzy told me, Jack, Mark and Colette and the other principals – Justine, Samantha, David and Xav to sit out. 'You aren't in the first dance,' she told us, 'so Stefan's going to be along in a moment to take you for a singing rehearsal.'

She split everyone else into two teams. 'These are the teams you'll be in for the performances,' she explained. She pointed to the group on her left. 'This side is the blue team. You'll have Sophie, Colette, Jack and Mark as your principals. The rest of you are the red team. You'll be with Justine, Samantha, David and Xav. Right, let's get started.'

First Dizzy demonstrated a series of steps and then everyone repeated them. When she was happy that everyone had mastered the steps, she turned on the tape player and they went through them to the music.

It was frightening how quickly the people in the chorus learnt the steps. Some of them only seemed to need to watch Dizzy once in order to pick up the dance. I began to feel worried. I was nowhere near as good.

Colette leaned over to me. 'It's all fairly easy stuff, isn't it?' she whispered confidently.

Easy! I forced a smile and nodded. 'Yeah, it looks fine.'

Just then Stefan came into the room. He beckoned for the eight of us to follow him outside.

'Looks like it's time for a music rehearsal,' Colette said to me. 'How's your singing?'

'OK,' I said, glad to be able to tell the truth.

Stefan took us upstairs to a music room with a piano. 'We're going to start with your first song,' he told us. 'It shows the four children being evacuated from London, travelling on the train and arriving at the house.'

He began by getting us to sing a series of scales. When he was happy that our voices were warmed up, we started on the song. It wasn't hard. Stefan sang a line and then we had to copy him. Once we'd got the basic tune sorted out, he listened to us one at a time. It was quite nerve-racking singing on my own but, to my relief, I didn't have any problems.

'You have a very good ear and a sweet voice,' Stefan smiled to me as I finished.

I blushed. Phew!

Most of the others had to go over their lines several times. Justine had the most problems. She just couldn't seem to get a couple of the notes. She had to repeat one line ten times before Stefan was happy.

By the time she had finished, she was looking very red. I felt sorry for her. I was probably going to be the same when it came to the dance rehearsal. I tried to give her a sympathetic look but she just stared at the floor, avoiding everyone's gaze.

Samantha, the girl who was playing Susan in Justine's group, was really good at singing. I remembered her from the auditions. She'd seemed OK then. However, as the rehearsal continued, it became clear that she really thought she was something special. She belted the song out and when she finished she smirked round at everyone as if to say, there, that's how it should be done. I began to go off her rapidly.

It soon became clear that I wasn't the only one who didn't like Samantha. The vibes between Colette and Samantha were definitely not good. Neither of them said a word to the other and when we left to go back to the theatre they totally ignored each other.

I hung back, intending to walk with Justine – she'd

been quiet ever since she'd had to sing on her own – but Colette came over. 'What are you doing?' she said. 'Come on. We're waiting for you.'

Seeing Mark and Jack standing by the door, I hesitated and then, deciding to speak to Justine at lunchtime, I joined my team. 'God, did you hear Samantha?' Colette said in a low voice to Mark as we walked down the stairs. 'She thinks she's so cool!'

'She *is* good at singing,' he said.

'Yeah, but there's no need to deafen us all,' Colette retorted.

Mark looked at me. 'Just ignore Colette when she gets on to the subject of Samantha. The two of them hate each other.'

'She hates me,' Colette said.

'Whatever,' Mark said, looking mildly exasperated.

'It's ever since last summer,' Colette told me. 'Our year did a production of *The Wizard of Oz*. She was Dorothy and I was her understudy. Well, on the week of the performance she got chickenpox and couldn't perform so I had to be Dorothy instead. Lots of people said I was better than her and she's hated me ever since.'

I nodded, not knowing what to say.

'She's been saying that in this play she's going to make sure her team's chosen to perform on the first night,' Colette said. 'So we've just got to be better than them, Sophie.'

'We will be,' Mark said. 'Sophie's going to be a much better Lucy than their Lucy.'

'Justine,' I said.

'Whatever her name is,' Mark went on, 'she really couldn't hold those notes.'

Colette smiled at me. 'I am *so* glad you're in our tcam, Sophic!'

I forced a smile.

I hoped she was still going to think that after we had our first dancing rehearsal!

✦

Chapter Eight

'Here we go!' Dizzy shouted above the music. 'And five, six, seven, eight . . .'

I ran forwards, aware of Colette, Mark and Jack in a line behind me. *Little steps, little steps*, I thought as I stopped and began to run on the spot.

To my right I could see Justine's team doing the same.

The music changed and I ran to a different area.

This wasn't hard at all. The only difficult thing was remembering when to run and when to stop. We were going to be dressed in hats and coats and carrying bags and we had to look like we were running from one place to another.

'That's great,' Dizzy said as the music ended. 'Well done, all of you.'

The breath rushed out of me. I hadn't made a mistake. Big relief!

'Time for lunch,' Dizzy announced. 'We'll meet back here at one thirty.'

*

We had all brought packed lunches and we ate them in the school canteen. Seeing Justine sitting by herself at a big table by the window, I headed over.

'Hi,' I said.

She smiled. 'Hi, Sophie. Do you want to sit here?'

'Yeah,' I replied.

But just then, Samantha, David and Xav came over.

David and Xav smiled at me but Samantha fixed me with a cold look. 'Your team's over there,' she said pointedly.

I looked round. Colette, Mark and Jack were sitting on the opposite side of the room. They beckoned me over.

'Well, are you going over to them?' Samantha said.

Could she have made it any clearer that I wasn't wanted?

I glanced at Justine but she just looked embarrassed and didn't say anything. Blushing, I picked up my lunch and walked over to Colette and the others. It wasn't fair. Samantha might not get on with Colette but why did she have to be mean to me too?

'What were you doing over there?' Colette asked.

'Nothing,' I muttered, sitting down.

'I wouldn't try and be friends with them,' Colette advised. 'Samantha's a real cow.'

Unpacking my sandwiches, I glanced across at the other team. Samantha caught my look and stared back challengingly. I looked quickly away. She really didn't seem to like me, that was for sure.

After lunch we learnt a dance that came halfway through the play when the children were having a feast with Aslan, the great lion.

Parts of the dance were very fast and I just couldn't seem to get my arms and legs moving together. The only trouble was, everyone else could.

After I had stumbled and got lost for the fourth time, Dizzy stopped everyone. 'Take five,' she called.

She came over to me. 'You seem to be having a problem, Sophie. Let's go through it.'

Dizzy took me through the sequence very closely, showing me every hand and arm movement. I had to repeat it several times but in the end I just about got it.

'That's better,' Dizzy said.

I glanced across the room. Colette, Jack and Mark were watching me curiously. I felt my face flush. 'Can I go now?' I asked.

Dizzy nodded. 'You mustn't worry if it takes you a little longer than some of the others to pick up the steps, you know, Sophie. You've had less formal training than anyone else. Just ask if you need help.'

'OK,' I mumbled, but inside I was shaking my head. I wasn't going to ask for extra help. There was no way I wanted to have to go over dances with the rest of the cast watching. It made me feel like a complete idiot.

I hurried over to Colette, Mark and Jack.

'Couldn't you get the sequence?' Colette said.

I shook my head.

'Never mind,' she said kindly. 'You'll soon pick it up. I can go through it again with you, if you like.'

'No, I'll be fine,' I said brightly. 'I've got it now.'

I hoped I was right.

When Dizzy called us back together, I managed the dance just about OK.

'See you tomorrow, Sophie,' Colette called as I picked up my bag at the end of rehearsal.

Justine came over to me. She looked a bit awkward and I could tell she was remembering what had happened at lunch. 'I've hardly seen you all day,' she said.

'It's been really busy, hasn't it?' I said.

'Yeah, but fun,' she replied. She hesitated. 'Though I didn't like the music rehearsal this morning.'

'And I didn't much like the dancing rehearsal after lunch,' I admitted. 'I was useless.' Somehow I felt I didn't have to pretend to be better than I was with Justine.

'You weren't as bad as me with the singing,' Justine said. 'I couldn't get the note at all.'

'You got it in the end,' I reassured her. 'You sounded really good. Much better than I was when I danced.'

'You'll work it out,' Justine said.

'Justine!' It was Samantha. 'Do you want to walk to the bus stop with me?'

'OK,' Justine replied. 'I'll see you tomorrow, Sophie.'

'Yeah,' I said. 'See you.' I smiled at Samantha but she ignored me.

She and Justine walked off. I hoisted my bag on to my shoulder. I had to be positive, I told myself. Justine was right. The dance was going to be fine. I just needed to practise, that was all.

When I got home, I rang Ally to find out whether she'd had any luck getting Harriet to talk about Kelly picking on her.

'No,' Ally sighed. 'She just kept changing the subject. I'm sure it'll blow over.'

'Yeah, I guess,' I said slowly.

'So how was your rehearsal?'

I told her about my day, and she told me how she and Harriet had gone out on a two-hour hack and then helped out with some of the little kids' riding lessons.

Finally Mum knocked on my door and said she needed me to get off the phone so she could use the internet.

Saying goodbye, I went downstairs. My tummy rumbled and I headed for the cupboard where the biscuits were kept. Yum! Jaffa Cakes. My favourite. I pulled out the box eagerly. It was strangely light. Opening it, I saw that someone – and I was betting it wasn't Mum or Dad – had eaten the Jaffa Cakes and slung the empty packet back. I sighed. Sometimes I could really dream about being an only child.

Just as I was throwing the empty packet into the bin, Dad and Tom came in. 'Did you eat all the Jaffa Cakes, Tom?' I demanded.

'Hi, Soph,' Tom said, ignoring my question. 'How's my favourite little sis', then?'

I stared at him. He sounded positively cheerful. 'What's up with you?' I asked suspiciously.

'He's had some good news,' Dad said, patting Snowy, who was leaping round his legs like a demented – and very fluffy – bouncy ball.

A broad grin split Tom's face. 'A guy from the Junction is going to come and hear the Blue Lemons play. If he likes us he said we can play at some of the Junction's under-eighteen nights. And we'll get paid!'

'That's brilliant!' I gasped, Jaffa Cakes forgotten. The Junction was a cool club in town. All Jessica and Tom's friends went there. 'When's he coming to watch you?'

'Two weeks,' Tom replied. He ran his hand through his hair enthusiastically. 'This could be the start of something. Something really big.'

'Well, as long as it doesn't interfere with your

schoolwork,' Dad warned. 'You know it's really important you do well in your GCSEs this year.'

'Yeah, yeah,' Tom said airily. He rolled his eyes at me, in a way that said *parents* and then he smiled. 'So, you want some Jaffa Cakes?' I nodded and he reached into his pocket. 'Tell you what, I'll go to the post office and buy you some, then.'

I almost fell through the floor in astonishment. Wow, he really *was* in a good mood.

The next day we had an acting rehearsal. Only the principals were called in and the room seemed very quiet compared to the day before. Claire began by showing us a model of the set with all the scenery.

'Now, get out your scripts,' she told us at last. 'We'll read through scene one and then block it.'

I knew from filming that blocking meant walking through the scene. Claire told us when and where to move and we had to write it in our scripts so that we wouldn't forget.

Justine's team blocked scene one while my team sat and watched and made notes.

'We'll swap over for the next scene,' Claire told us.

It was odd hearing Justine reading out Lucy's words. She said some of the lines differently from how I would have. Sometimes she sounded happy when I thought Lucy would be more thoughtful and sometimes she just seemed to put the wrong emphasis on the words.

When it was my team's turn to block scene two, I jumped out of my chair eagerly. I couldn't wait to have a go. In the second scene the children explore the house and find the wardrobe which eventually leads them to the magical land of Narnia. I think I did quite well. Claire certainly seemed pleased.

'That was excellent, Sophie,' she told me. 'You really seem to have got under the skin of Lucy. You actually made me believe in her. Well done.'

For a moment I wondered if Claire was just being nice because I was the youngest, but then I realized that she hadn't praised Justine in the same way in the scene before.

My doubts were further pushed away when Claire told us to take a ten-minute break, and Colette and the boys hurried over.

'That was really good, Sophie!' Colette exclaimed. 'You were just like Lucy should be.'

'Yeah, you were great,' Jack said, looking really impressed. 'I felt like you were really my little sister.'

'We're so lucky to have you as our Lucy,' Colette said, shooting a look in the other team's direction. 'Justine's nowhere near as good as you.'

I could feel myself glowing. It was brilliant to have Colette and the others looking really pleased to have me in their team again. I made a resolution. From now on, that was the way it was going to stay.

Chapter Nine

'The Junction!' Ally exclaimed, when I announced Tom's news the next day on our way into school. She's really into music and I knew she'd be very impressed. 'That's so cool!'

'What's the Junction?' Harriet asked.

'It's a club in town. It does under-eighteen nights,' I explained. 'Jessica and her friends go. You have to be at least fourteen to get in.'

'So, when's this guy coming to see them?' Ally asked.

'Two weeks,' I replied.

Harriet giggled. She looked definitely unimpressed. 'I wonder what Tom and his mates will wear. I bet they'll look really stupid.'

I grinned at her. 'Of course. I mean it *is* Tom we're talking about.'

Just then, Eve from Ally's class came into the cloak-room.

'Hi, Eve,' Ally said. 'You'll never guess what – Sophie was just telling us that the band her brother Tom is in might get to play at the Junction.'

'Wow!' Eve said, looking at me. 'That's brilliant! My cousin's in a band and they used to play there. He's gone to university now.'

'Your cousin's in a band?' Ally questioned, looking interested. 'What's it called?'

'The Scream,' Eve replied. 'They're really good. They've just got a record deal.' She hung up her coat. 'They're doing some gigs around here at Christmas time. One of them's for charity at our village hall.' She looked almost shyly at Ally. 'I could try and get you a ticket as well if you like.'

'Yeah!' Ally said eagerly.

Eve smiled at her. 'Are you coming into the classroom?'

Ally hesitated and looked at Harriet and me. She had got into the habit of coming into our classroom before morning registration. 'Umm . . . yeah, I guess. I'll . . . er, see you two later.'

Watching Ally head off with Eve felt strange.

'Eve seems nice, doesn't she?' Harriet said slowly.

'Yeah,' I agreed, feeling weird. 'Yeah, she does.'

We walked towards our classroom. 'So, when's your next rehearsal?' Harriet asked me.

'Tomorrow night,' I replied. 'It's another dancing rehearsal, worse luck.'

Harriet looked at me sympathetically. I'd told her all about being picked out on Saturday as we'd travelled to school on the bus. 'You'll get better at the dancing,' she said comfortingly. 'You just need to practise.'

I nodded in determination. *Yes,* I thought. *That's all I need to do.*

Over the next two weeks I practised and practised. Every night after school I went over the dances and, to my relief, I seemed to be managing to keep up with the others. But then, one Tuesday night, Dizzy broke the news about Lucy's ballet solo.

'OK, tonight you're going to start learning your solo,' she said to me and Justine as everyone else took a drinks' break.

'Solo?' I echoed.

Dizzy nodded. 'It comes in the scene at Mr Tumnus's house. After you have had tea you dance a kind of ballet.'

'Cool!' Justine said, looking really pleased. 'I love ballet.'

I gulped. This sounded difficult.

Dizzy seemed to see the worry on my face. 'Don't look like that, Sophie; you'll manage just fine. Although it's going to be based on ballet-style move-ments I'm not expecting either of you to look like trained ballet dancers. In fact, what I want you to look like is a little girl dancing naturally out of sheer joy.' She went to the tape player. 'Now I'll play you the music and show you the dance.'

I felt slightly better. And then I saw Dizzy dance.

As she spun and jumped my mouth dropped open. I was going to have to do *that*? It was impossible. There were pirouettes, lots of jumps and an arabesque — that's where you balance on one leg with the other leg out behind you. I was *never* going to be able to do it.

As the music ended and Dizzy spun to a halt, her arms outstretched, the watching dancers all clapped and cheered and a few of the boys wolf-whistled. She grinned at them. 'OK, OK, settle down, guys.' Then she turned to Justine and me. 'Right, now it's your turn.'

I felt rooted to the ground in horror. She wanted me to do *that* — in front of everyone!

I swallowed. This was a nightmare. It had to be a nightmare.

'You start over here, feet in fifth position,' Dizzy instructed. 'Come on, Sophie,' she called as Justine eagerly hurried over and stood in fifth position, her right foot neatly placed in front of her left, her toes turned out.

I walked towards them, feeling sick.

'So, from fifth position,' Dizzy said, walking slowly through the first sequence of steps, 'you start with a simple *glissande derrière*, so that's *a demi-plié*, slide your left foot to second position, raise your left foot and spring, as you land stretch your right foot off the ground and then slide it back to a *demi-plié* in fifth . . .'

What? I stood motionless as Justine followed the instructions easily.

'Come on, Sophie, what are you waiting for?' Dizzy frowned.

It took me four attempts to get that first sequence even vaguely right.

'It's not that hard,' Dizzy told me. 'Just try and relax.'

Relax? With everyone watching me?

'OK, and on to the next sequence,' Dizzy said. 'It's an *assemblé dessus* followed by two *changements*.'

It was the worst fifteen minutes of my life. I just couldn't get the dance at all. It was partly because it was quite difficult and partly because I could feel everyone watching. As I made mistake after mistake, I got more and more tense and that made my dancing even worse. I saw people whispering to each other. I was sure they were talking about me.

'OK, maybe we'll call it a day for now,' Dizzy said, to my utter relief. 'Justine, that was great. Just remember to keep your body as straight as possible in the *changements*. Sophie,' she turned to me, a slight frown on her face, 'I'll go through it again with you on Sunday. You're obviously finding it difficult. But don't worry. You'll get it in the end – it's really not that hard.'

I wanted to drop through the floor with embarrassment.

'Off you go and sit down now,' Dizzy said.

I hurried back to my seat, my cheeks burning.

Justine caught up with me. 'Sophie. Wait!'

I stopped.

'Look,' she said sympathetically. 'I know you haven't done much ballet. If you want you can come to my house and we can . . .'

'Way to go, Justine!' Samantha interrupted, hurrying over. 'You looked brilliant!' She glanced at me and there was a triumphant smirk on her face. 'Guess we know now which team's going to be picked to perform on opening night.'

I'd thought I couldn't feel any worse. But I'd been wrong.

'Come on, Jus,' Samantha said to Justine. 'Come and sit with me, David and Xav. We're going through our lines in the first scene.' Justine looked at me but Samantha linked arms with her. 'Come on!' she insisted.

I slowly made my way back to where Colette, Jack and Mark were sitting. 'That didn't look much fun,' Jack said, giving me a wry smile.

'No,' I muttered.

'You'll pick it up,' Colette said breezily, but I heard a note of worry in her voice. Oh great; she thought I was going to let the team down too.

Picking up my script, I pretended to study my lines but the words blurred as I blinked away the tears of humiliation prickling my eyes.

Thankfully the rest of the rehearsal wasn't too bad. When the chorus had finished learning the dance in the Queen's palace we all started learning moves for the big battle scene. Although it was set to music, it was more like acting than dancing and as I pretended to be Lucy in the midst of the battle I felt myself starting to relax. The moves came easily and by the time we finished for the night I was actually enjoying myself.

'That was more like it,' Dizzy said, coming over to me as everyone started to get their bags. 'When you relax you dance really well, Sophie. Now, go home and I'll see you on the weekend.'

I headed for the door. I could see Mum in the foyer. I had just reached her when Velda came up to me.

'Sophie, I've had calls from journalists who've heard about you being Lucy in the play. They know about you being in the film and they want to do articles on you, if that's OK?'

If it was OK! Excitement leapt inside me at the thought of being interviewed. 'Yeah . . . yeah, it's fine,' I replied.

'Which papers are they from?' Mum asked.

Velda checked her clipboard. 'It's the two local papers – the *Loughborough Echo* and the *Nottingham Evening Post*. I'll try and arrange it so that they both interview Sophie on Saturday.'

'How exciting,' Mum said to me.

'I'm sure they won't be the only interviews Sophie has to do,' Velda told her. 'There are bound to be magazine and radio interviews nearer the time too. It's a good story – local girl comes from nowhere to take the lead in a film and then gets the main part in a big Christmas show. It'll be great publicity for us. People are bound to want to come and see the local film star. Anyway, see you on Saturday, Sophie.'

I nodded. Velda's words had made my stomach suddenly go all squirmy. Not the bit about seeing me on Saturday of course, but her comment that lots of people were going to come and see the play because of me. Help! They'd all be expecting me to be perfect. But what about my dancing? What if I made a total mess of things on stage?

I followed Mum to the car feeling almost sick.

'Sophie?' Mum frowned as we got into the car. 'Are you OK? You're being very quiet.'

'I . . . I'm fine,' I mumbled.

'Are you sure?' Mum asked, looking at me closely.

I nodded. I didn't want to talk about it. 'I'm just tired,' I lied.

To my relief Mum seemed to accept this. 'It is late,

isn't it?' she said. 'And you've got school tomorrow. Come on, let's go home.'

'It's going to be really strange being interviewed,' I said to Ally and Harriet the next day as we sat on the wall at breaktime.

'Yeah,' Harriet said. 'But I guess you're going to have to get used to it. When the film comes out you're probably going to be asked to do loads of interviews.'

'Maybe you'll be on TV,' Ally said. 'You know, something like SMTV.'

Weird! But I knew she was right. I really could be on telly. I felt like pinching myself. It was hard to believe how much my life had changed in the last few months. I opened my mouth, about to admit to Ally and Harriet how worried I felt about people coming to watch me thinking I was going to be perfect, but just then Eve came over and I changed my mind.

'Hi,' she said, smiling at us all. 'Ally, I've just seen Nikita, you know, the sixth former who organizes the art club. We're doing papier mâché or something this lunchtime and she said she needs help tearing up lots of newspaper. I'm going to go and give her a hand – do you want to come?'

'OK,' Ally replied, jumping off the wall.

'Matthew's helping too – and Nathan,' Eve told her.

'Cool!' Ally exclaimed.

Eve grinned. 'I thought you might think that!'

So Ally had told Eve about liking Nathan. I'd thought only Harriet and I knew. The thought of Ally talking to Eve and sharing secrets made me feel decidedly odd.

'See you later,' Ally called to Harriet and me, and she hurried off with Eve in the direction of the Art block.

For a moment, neither Harriet or I said anything. I had the distinct feeling that Harriet was feeling just as strange as I was about watching Ally and Eve go off together.

'Well . . . um, fancy testing me on quiz questions?' Harriet said at last.

'Sure,' I shrugged, trying to stop thinking about Ally having a new friend.

'So, how's the quiz club going?' I asked as she rummaged in her bag and pulled out her quiz book.

Harriet's eyes lit up. 'I love it! It's such fun, you learn loads and everyone's really nice.'

I smiled. 'Especially someone whose name begins with B?'

Harriet went pink. 'I really like him. He's so clever and . . .'

I nudged her quickly. 'Ssh!'

Ben was walking along the path towards us.

'Say hello when he comes past!' I hissed.

Harriet started to shake her head. 'No! I can't!'

'Go on!' I insisted.

Harriet took a deep breath but just as she opened her mouth, Kelly, Leanne and Rachel came up the path in the other direction.

'Ben,' Kelly said. 'Hi!' Leaving Leanne and Rachel, she hurried over to him.

'Oh, hi, Kelly,' Ben said. Phew! He didn't sound that delighted to see her.

'How are you?' Kelly asked, smiling up at him.

She was pretty but, to my relief, Ben just gave a half smile back. 'Fine, thanks. Look, I've . . . er, really got to –'

'Have you been doing much sailing?' Kelly interrupted him.

'Yeah, a bit,' he answered. He spoke politely but his eyes flickered around as if he wanted to get away.

'Have you seen that new movie with Brad Pitt in, the one where he tries to sail across that ocean?'

'No,' he replied.

'Neither have I.' Kelly ran her fingers through her hair and looked at him hopefully. When he didn't say anything, she added, 'Maybe we could go together?'

'Maybe. Look, I've really got go,' Ben said quickly. 'See you around, Kelly.' He hurried past her – and us.

Disappointment crossed Kelly's face.

Leanne and Rachel hurried up to her. 'Did you ask him out?' Leanne asked.

'Sort of,' Kelly said. 'But he didn't say anything. He

just dashed off.' She tossed her hair back. 'Oh well, he's not the only boy in this school.'

'Yeah, forget him,' Rachel advised.

Kelly nodded. 'Let's go in.'

Suddenly she caught sight of Harriet and me. 'What are you looking at?' she demanded, and I could see her realizing that we must have heard her whole conversation with Ben.

I just shrugged but Harriet went red. 'Nothing,' she stammered.

Kelly looked her up and down. 'Love the socks, Harriet!' she said sarcastically.

'So cool!' Leanne said with a giggle.

Harriet was wearing a pair of old socks – navy blue but with *I love ponies* written round the ankle in red writing. She'd had them since about Year Four.

'It's the way your trousers stop just above the ankle,' Kelly went on, and I could tell she was just having a go at Harriet because she was still fed up about Ben turning her down. 'It shows them off perfectly.'

'You never know, maybe you'll start a new trend,' Rachel said.

'Or maybe not,' Kelly added.

'Oh shut up,' I told them.

Snorting with laughter, Kelly, Rachel and Leanne went into the building.

I looked at Harriet. Her face was bright red. 'Just ignore them,' I said. 'They're morons.'

'Yeah,' she muttered in a small voice. 'Yeah — you're right.'

But despite what Harriet said, she couldn't seem to ignore Kelly. For the rest of the week Kelly continued to tease her. It was really bad on Friday when Kelly saw Ben talking to Harriet after they had come out from a quiz club meeting together.

'Ooh, got a boyfriend have you, Harriet?' she mocked as Harriet came over to meet me afterwards.

Harriet went the colour of a tomato.

'Does he like your big granny pants?' Kelly sniggered. 'I bet he finds them *really* attractive.'

'Ben isn't my boyfriend,' Harriet said quickly.

Kelly burst out laughing as if Harriet had said the funniest thing ever. 'I was *joking*.' She snorted. 'As if Ben would go out with someone like you.'

'You can talk,' I said. 'I didn't exactly notice Ben jumping at the chance of going to the cinema with you, Kelly. Or has he changed his mind?' Seeing Kelly's expression darken, I grabbed Harriet's arm. 'Thought not. Come on, Harriet, let's go.'

I marched off, half dragging Harriet beside me.

Honestly, Kelly could be so annoying at times!

★

Chapter Ten

'I've heard there're some journalists coming in!' Justine said to me when I arrived at rehearsal on Saturday morning. 'They want to talk to you and me about being Lucy.'

I hesitated. That wasn't the way Velda had put it on Tuesday – she'd made it sound like the journalists just wanted to interview me.

'It's really exciting, isn't it?' Justine went on. 'Let's go and find Velda and ask her exactly when they'll be here.'

Velda was looking at the stage plans. 'Velda,' Justine said, bouncing up to her. 'What time are the journalists coming in?'

'At twelve,' Velda answered. She smiled at me. 'There're three journalists now. There's one coming in from *Sugar* magazine too.'

Sugar! Wow. Just wait till Ally and Harriet heard that!

'Will they take our photographs?' Justine asked eagerly.

Velda looked surprised. 'Your photograph?' Realization dawned on her face. 'Oh, they're not interviewing you, Justine. Just Sophie. I'm sorry. Did you think you were being interviewed too?'

Justine blushed. 'Ur . . . yeah.' She looked like she wanted to drop through the floor with embarrassment.

I felt awful for her. 'Couldn't they interview us both?' I asked quickly.

Velda shrugged. 'I could suggest it to them. But I think the reason they want to interview you, Sophie, is because you were the lead in the film.'

'But Justine was in the film too and we are both Lucy,' I said.

Velda nodded. 'I'll see what they say.'

I glanced at Justine. 'I . . . I'm going to get a drink,' she mumbled.

I went after her. 'I'm sure they will want to interview you as well,' I said.

'It doesn't matter,' Justine muttered, her face still pink. 'I don't care.'

But it was obvious that she cared loads. We poured ourselves drinks in an uncomfortable silence.

'Hi, Justine,' Samantha said, coming over and totally ignoring me as usual. 'Should we go through our lines together?'

'OK,' Justine said. And, looking relieved to get away from me, she hurried off with Samantha.

*

I had a good day. The acting rehearsal went well and the interviews were fun. The only downside was that Justine wasn't interviewed. Velda was right. The journalists just wanted to talk to me. When I was called to the interviews Justine shot me a jealous look, and when I came back she avoided me completely. I felt bad but I didn't see there was much I could do. After all, I couldn't *make* the journalists interview her.

'I can't believe you're going to be in *Sugar*,' Ally said that evening. She and Harriet had called round after riding. 'That is so cool!'

'And you're going to be in the local papers too,' Harriet said, stroking Billy, our new doggy guest. He was a beautiful but very greedy Golden Retriever. Plonking his head on Harriet's knee, he gazed up at the biscuit she was munching with hopeful brown eyes. Mum's new business was certainly going well. She had pets booked in almost every week until Christmas.

Dad turned from the sink where he was washing up. 'Did the journalists say when the articles would come out, Sophie?'

'The local papers said some time in the next few weeks,' I replied, feeding Billy a bit of my biscuit. 'The journalist from *Sugar* said it would be in the December issue.' I got up. 'Can we have some crisps as well, Dad?'

Dad nodded. 'But just one packet. We'll be eating as soon as I've taken Tom to Nick's house.'

'They're playing at the hall in Nick's village tonight,' I told Ally and Harriet. 'The talent spotter from the Junction's coming to see them.'

Dad checked his watch. 'And they're going to be late if they're not careful.' He went to the door. 'Tom! Are you coming?'

Tom came downstairs with his electric guitar. I stared.

OK, now I know he normally looks weird but this time he had outdone himself. His hair was gelled into points, chains were strung from his pockets to his waist and he was wearing about ten bracelets on each wrist. As a finishing touch he had painted his fingernails black.

I saw Dad do a double take. 'Well,' he said, blinking.

'What?' Tom challenged him.

'Are you really going out like that?' Dad struggled. He doesn't normally like coming down the heavy-handed parent on us but I could tell even he was taken aback by Tom's appearance.

'Yes,' Tom said. 'Why?'

'You look a bit . . . er . . . a bit extreme,' Dad said.

'Dad!' Tom rolled his eyes. 'We're in a *band*.'

'Yes, but there's no need to look quite as . . .' Dad seemed lost for words.

'Stupid?' I put in helpfully. Harriet giggled and even Ally smiled.

'Sophie,' Dad said warningly. He looked back at Tom. 'Maybe you should tone it down a bit, mate.'

'There's nothing to tone down. I look fine, Dad,' Tom said in exasperation.

Dad looked like he was going to argue but then he just sighed. 'OK. If you think so.' He picked up the car keys. 'Come on, let's go.'

They walked out.

As soon as the door was shut I began to giggle. 'Can you believe what Tom looks like?'

'I know,' Harriet agreed. 'And he seems to think he looks cool.'

'He didn't look *that* bad,' Ally said defensively, seeming to forget that even she had been smirking when she'd first seen him. 'And it'll be amazing if the Junction want his band though, won't it?'

'Amazingly unlikely,' I grinned.

'They're good,' Ally persisted. 'They might get picked. And if they play at the Junction they might get discovered and become a real band.' Ally looked excited. 'They could be on *Top of the Pops*.'

Yeah, as if!

Harriet checked her watch. 'I should go. Dad's expecting me home soon.'

'I should go too,' Ally said. 'Good luck at the rehearsal tomorrow, Soph.'

'Thanks,' I sighed. 'I think I'm going to need it.'

*

'And spin and reach and hold it there!' An approving look spread across Dizzy's face. 'That's much better, Sophie,' she said. 'And relax.'

I lowered my arms.

'That was a definite improvement,' Dizzy said. 'You still need to sort out the *pas de chat* jumps but those will come right with practice.'

I felt a rush of relief. Dizzy had asked me to come in early to go through the ballet with her. It was so much easier to dance with just Dizzy. I didn't mind going over and over each move if there was no one else watching.

'I'll go through it with you and Justine again after lunch,' Dizzy told me. 'Now go and put your shoes on; the others should be here in a minute.'

I sat down and pulled my shoes back on – the ballet dance was going to be done barefoot and Dizzy had decided that it would be good to start practising barefoot right from the start. As I stood up, the others started to arrive.

That morning we were working on the final company number. There were some quite difficult bits and I stayed near the back to avoid Dizzy's eagle eye.

'Are you OK on that last sequence, Sophie?' she asked as she watched us do the dance in groups.

'I'm fine,' I told her.

To my relief she nodded and turned away.

'Didn't look like it to me,' I heard Samantha say.

She was in the row behind me. 'You messed up that second spin,' she said to me, her eyes appraising. 'Dizzy just didn't see.'

Colette was standing to my left. 'Shut up, Samantha. You don't know what you're talking about.'

'Don't I?' Samantha raised her eyebrows. 'Look, why don't you just accept it, Colette? Our team's going to be much better than yours. At least *we* can all dance.'

Colette's eyes flashed. 'And at least we can all act, or had you conveniently forgotten how important that is? It wouldn't surprise me. After all, acting's never been your strong point, has it, Samantha?'

Two spots of bright colour jumped into Samantha's cheeks. 'I can act!'

'Quieten down over there,' Dizzy called and, glaring at each other, Colette and Samantha shut up.

Colette walked off and I edged over to Justine. 'Hi,' I said tentatively. I hadn't spoken to her that morning and I had the distinct impression that she was still avoiding me.

'Oh, hi,' she said shortly.

I wanted to make friends again. 'Look . . .'

'Justine,' Samantha interrupted me. 'Let's go and get a drink.' She looked witheringly at me. 'Go and join your own team, Sophie. We don't want you hanging around with us.'

I felt like she'd slapped me. 'What?' I stammered.

Samantha stepped closer and glared at me. 'Listen, it's our team against your team, which means you're not wanted here.' She looked at Justine. 'Isn't that right, Justine?'

'Well . . . er . . .' Justine looked uncomfortable. 'Umm . . .'

I stared at her. Was she really not going to stand up to Samantha?

'See?' Samantha said to me.

'Fine,' I retorted. 'I'm going!'

Feeling very annoyed with Justine, I marched away, my head held high. So high that I didn't happen to see the bag on the floor in front of me.

'Oof!' I gasped, as I tripped flat on my face.

Samantha hooted with laughter and Justine giggled.

You know when you just want the ground to open and swallow you up? Right then I just wanted to *die*.

'Great work, everyone. We'll break for lunch now,' Dizzy eventually announced. 'Sophie and Justine, I want you ready to start again at one thirty to go through your ballet solo.'

As I sat down with Colette, I noticed Samantha looking across at me and saying something to her team, a grin on her face. I had a feeling they were talking about the ballet solo.

I tried to ignore them but I couldn't. I glanced over again. Samantha was now whispering intently, a gleam in her eyes. I saw Justine start to shake her head and protest but Samantha quickly interrupted her.

'What do you think they're talking about?' I said uneasily, as I saw the boys look in my direction and grin.

'Who cares?' Colette said, glancing briefly at them. 'Just ignore them.'

After lunch I went to warm up. To my surprise, Justine came over to me. 'Hi,' she said tentatively.

'Hello,' I replied shortly, wondering what she wanted.

'You know you've been slipping on the jumps in the ballet,' she said.

I nodded.

'Well, maybe these will help.' She held out two socks made out of tights material. 'They're called dance socks and they're really good at stopping you slipping. We use them all the time in dance classes. Here, take them,' she offered.

I looked at her suspiciously. I couldn't forget how she'd been that morning. 'Why are you letting me use them?'

Justine shrugged. 'I . . . I just feel bad about earlier. Samantha shouldn't have told you to go away like that.' She blushed. 'I want to be friends.'

My bad mood lifted. OK, so maybe she wasn't so bad after all.

'Thanks,' I smiled, taking the socks. They were the

same colour as my skin. I put them on and stood up. You could hardly see them on my feet but they made me feel like a proper dancer. I pointed my toe experimentally. The floor seemed to glide beneath it.

'Sophie!' Dizzy called from the CD player. 'Are you ready?'

I nodded and walked over.

'Let's take it from the top,' she instructed.

I could see the other principals all gathering to watch what I was doing. *Here goes*, I thought, taking up the starting position. *And into fifth position*, I thought, my feet sliding easily across the floor in the dance socks, *arms up and spring . . .*

My feet slipped from underneath me and I landed in a heap on the floor. 'Ow!' I gasped.

I heard a few muffled giggles and turned. Samantha and the rest of the red team were grinning in delight. Even Justine was smiling. My warm feelings for her disappeared in a flash.

'Doing well, Sophie,' Samantha called.

Dizzy shot her an annoyed look. 'That's enough, Samantha!'

Red in the face, I stood up.

'What happened there?' Dizzy called to me. 'You seemed to lose your balance completely.'

'I . . . I don't know,' I replied.

'Try again. Just from the jump. And five, six, seven, eight!'

114

As I started the side step into the first jump my feet slipped on the floor.

'Hang on, Sophie. Stop!' Dizzy shouted.

I stopped. 'What have you got on your feet?' she demanded, walking over to me and staring at my toes.

'Dance socks,' I said uncertainly.

'Dance socks?' Dizzy raised her eyebrows. 'And *what* are dance socks?'

I stared at her. What did she mean — what are dance socks? She was a dance teacher. And then I heard the red team's sniggers and it hit me. It was a joke. Justine had tricked me!

'Um . . . er,' I stammered.

'Take them off,' Dizzy said abruptly.

I quickly removed them. 'Well, I don't know who's being telling you that these are dance socks,' Dizzy said, shaking her head as she looked at them. 'But it's lucky you didn't break your ankle. Dancing in these would be like trying to dance on ice.' She looked at me. 'So, who told you to wear them?'

I ached to tell her the truth but I wasn't going to drop Justine in it — no matter how much I wanted to. I looked at the floor.

'I see,' Dizzy said after a moment. 'Well, I advise you to no longer listen to whoever told you to wear them. Now, let's try the dance again — this time *without* the socks.'

But the fall had put me off and it took me ages to get the dance even vaguely right.

'Let's leave it there,' Dizzy said at last, to my relief. 'Justine, your turn now.'

I went slowly back to my team. They were looking confused.

'Have a good trip?' Samantha grinned as I walked past.

David and Xav laughed.

I felt myself go red. How *could* I have been so stupid to have been taken in like that? I should have known it was a trick.

'Let me know if you want to borrow some dance socks again,' Samantha said. 'I haven't laughed so much in ages!'

I saw Colette's eyes widen as she put two and two together. 'You gave Sophie those socks?'

'Well, Justine did, but it was my idea,' Samantha said. 'Good joke, wasn't it?'

'Joke? She could really have hurt herself!' Colette said angrily.

'It was a stupid thing to do!' Jack said.

'Oh, lighten up,' Samantha drawled.

'Quiet over there!' Dizzy called.

We all shut up. 'Stupid idiots!' Colette whispered to me. 'Are you OK?'

I nodded. But inside I was still smarting. It had been a mean trick to play and I felt totally betrayed by

Justine. OK, so maybe she was jealous that I'd got to be interviewed and she hadn't, and the trick had been Samantha's idea not hers, but she needn't have gone along with it. Anger and hurt surged through me. To think I'd imagined we might actually be friends. Huh! I should have known better than to trust Justine Wilcox.

After Justine had danced – effortlessly, of course – through the solo, Dizzy announced that we were going to go through all the dances that we had learnt so far.

'I want to get an idea of how all the dances are looking and how well you are remembering them,' she told us. 'So we'll go through them without stopping.'

While the rest of the chorus danced the opening number, I took my place with the other principals at the side. Samantha smirked at me. I could tell she thought I was going to mess up and my heart sank.

Samantha was right. I managed the first few dances OK but then I got completely lost in the beaver dance, and in the celebration of Aslan's return I was late on almost every spin.

Around me the rest of the cast seemed to be spinning and jumping perfectly, every movement right on time. I could feel myself blushing. I caught Dizzy looking at me. *Try harder*, I urged myself.

'Take a ten-minute break and then we'll go through each dance slowly,' Dizzy told us at the end.

Everyone started to stand up. As I got to my feet, I saw Dizzy heading towards me. Oh no. She was going to say something about how awful I'd been. She was going to tell me I needed extra help. Maybe she was even going to make me go through the dances now on my own in front of everyone.

I couldn't cope.

'Sophie . . .' Dizzy started to say.

'I've got to go to the bathroom,' I blurted out and I hurried to the door that led to the toilets.

Sally and Natalie, two of the really good dancers, were standing by the sinks adjusting their hair. 'That was OK, wasn't it?' I heard Sally say as I quickly shut myself in one of the cubicles. 'I forgot a few bits but it wasn't that bad for a first run-through of all those dances.'

'No,' Natalie agreed. 'And Dizzy seemed pleased.'

I rested my head against the cold plastic door and wished I could be them. I had made so many mistakes. What was Dizzy going to say to me? I began to wish I could stay in the cubicle for ever.

I stayed there until I was sure the drinks' break was over. When I sidled back into the auditorium Dizzy had already started going through the first dance – the one I wasn't in – taking each sequence of steps slowly and making sure that everyone was moving in time.

Colette was sitting with Jack and Mark but I couldn't bring myself to go and join them. I sat down by myself. Oh help, what was I going to do?

Chapter Eleven

'I bet it wasn't that bad,' Ally said to me the next morning on the bus as I told her and Harriet about how awful the rehearsal had been. 'I know the trick Justine played was really mean but I bet your dancing was OK really.'

'It wasn't,' I replied gloomily. 'Even without the socks I made loads of mistakes.'

'Can't you just ask for more help?' Harriet said.

'No.'

'Why not?' Harriet frowned.

'I just can't.' I tried to explain. 'Everyone expects me to be good. You know, having been in a film. They'll think I'm really stupid.'

'But you didn't have to dance in the film,' Harriet pointed out. 'Sophie, it's silly not asking for help if you need it just because of what other people might think. Isn't it better to ask for help rather than just to go on making mistakes?'

'Yes . . . no . . .' I could just imagine how Samantha and Justine would laugh if Dizzy gave me extra help. And then there were Colette and Jack and

Mark. What would they think? 'It's not that easy.'

'It *is* that easy.' Harriet frowned. 'Just ask for help.'

'I bet you're just stressing about nothing,' Ally said airily. 'You'll be fine. I'm really looking forward to coming to see it. Mum said she's going to buy tickets for the first night.'

'Dad's getting me and Emily tickets for the first night too,' Harriet said. 'We should make sure we get seats near to each other.'

'But I don't know if I'll be performing on the first night yet,' I said quickly. 'It depends which team's the best.'

'It's going to be your team,' Ally said. 'There's no way Justine's going to be chosen over you.'

'Yeah,' Harriet agreed. 'You're loads better than Justine.'

Hadn't they been listening to a word I'd been saying? 'But . . .'

Ally interrupted. 'So, anyway, how did Tom's band do at the weekend? Did the guy from the Junction like them?'

I gave up trying to talk about the play. They just didn't understand. 'Yeah,' I replied. Tom had been really excited when he'd got in from the gig. I'd been in bed but he, Jessica, Mum and Dad had made such a noise in the kitchen that I'd gone downstairs. 'He's asked them to play in December.'

'Oh wow!' Ally gasped, causing the people in front

of us to glance round curiously. She ignored them. 'That's so cool! We have to go and watch them.'

'Small problem – we're not fourteen,' I pointed out.

'We could look it if we put lots of make-up on,' Ally said.

'Yeah, right,' I said. I'm sorry but what planet was she on? There was about as much chance of the bouncers at the Junction believing that we were all fourteen as there was of me being able to dance perfectly by the time the play opened. In other words, no chance at all.

Before lunch we had PE. As Harriet pulled off her trousers I saw that she had different knickers on from usual. They were plain white, but they were high leg ones just like me and Ally and most other people wore. I stared. I'd never seen Harriet wearing knickers like that before.

It wasn't the only surprise in store for me. As Harriet unbuttoned her school shirt I saw that she was wearing a bra. Not a crop top. A bra!

I didn't want to say anything in the changing room with people like Kelly listening but as soon as we set off for the hockey pitch, I caught Harriet's arm. 'You've got a bra!' I whispered.

She looked embarrassed. 'Yeah – so?'

'When? Why didn't you tell me?'

'I got it on Saturday. I went into town.'

'But who with?' My eyes widened. 'Not your dad?' Harriet's mum and dad are divorced and she hardly ever sees her mum. She gets on really well with her dad but going to buy a bra with him – no, that would just be too embarrassing.

'I went on my own,' she said. 'Dad dropped me off at Marks & Spencer – he had some stuff to get at B & Q and he let me go shopping there. I used my allowance.'

I stared at her. I would have thought she would have been way too embarrassed to go and get a bra on her own. I certainly would have been – particularly in a place like Marks & Spencer. The underwear department there is seriously scary, with all sorts of lace and satin and lots of women wandering around.

'I can't believe you went on your own,' I said. I was struck by a practicality. 'How did you know what size to get?'

'I didn't,' Harriet confessed, 'I was about to guess when this sales lady came up to me and asked me if I wanted to be measured.'

I stared at her in horror. 'What did you say?' I squeaked.

'I said yes.' Harriet blushed. 'It was really embarrassing but at least it meant I got the right size.'

I stared at her. It was as if the Harriet I knew had disappeared in front of my eyes. This was a new Harriet, a different one.

'It's not such a big deal,' Harriet said, looking awkward.

Not a big deal! To go into a underwear department on your own to buy a bra and to be measured by a sales lady. I was almost struck dumb with astonishment. Almost but not quite. 'Why didn't you say anything? Why didn't you tell me and Ally?'

Harriet shrugged. 'I didn't see the point.'

We reached the hockey field. 'Come on, girls. Stop dawdling!' Miss Fraser strode towards us. 'We haven't got all day. Warm up with a lap round the field, and no walking or you'll be going round twice!'

At lunchtime I really wanted to talk to Ally about it. There was just one problem: I couldn't exactly talk to her with Harriet there. However, to my relief, Harriet gave me the opportunity herself.

'I've got some wine gums in my coat pocket,' she said, as we left the dining hall. 'Shall I go and get them?'

'Yeah!' I said, seizing the chance to speak to Ally on her own.

'We'll come with you,' Ally said to Harriet.

'No,' I said quickly, grabbing her arm. 'Let's wait here. It's such a nice day.' Of course that excuse would have worked better if it *had* actually been a nice day.

Ally stared at the grey clouds lowering overhead. 'It is?' she said.

'I need some fresh air,' I said hastily. 'Stay with me, Ally. You don't mind, do you Harriet?'

'No, that's fine,' Harriet said, thankfully not seeming to see the meaningful looks I was shooting at Ally. 'I'll be back in a few minutes.'

She set off.

Ally looked at me curiously. 'So what's going on?'

'It's Harriet,' I said, lowering my voice. 'Did you know she's got a . . .'

I stopped as Eve came running up to us.

'Ally, I've been looking for you! You'll never guess what. Matthew's just asked me out!'

'What?' Ally squealed. 'What did you say?'

'Yes, of course!' Eve replied. 'We're going out at the weekend to the cinema.' She grinned. 'This could work out so well. After all, who's Matthew's best friend?'

'Nathan!' Ally said.

'Yeah!' Eve exclaimed. 'Maybe he'll ask you out and we can go on a double date or something.'

'Ohmigod!' Ally squeaked. 'That would be perfect!'

They began to chatter away about Nathan and Matthew. I couldn't join in so I just sat on the wall and waited for Harriet.

'You're quiet,' Jessica said as we walked home together. 'What's up?'

'Nothing,' I muttered.

'Are you sure?' Jess probed.

'It's just Harriet – and Ally,' I confessed. 'Things are odd at the moment. There's these girls picking on Harriet and she's getting upset by it and –' I hesitated; this was going to sound really dumb – 'well, Ally's got a new friend in her class and she seems to have less and less time to spend with Harriet and me.'

I half expected Jessica to laugh and tell me to stop being so stupid but she didn't. She looked at me sympathetically. 'Things change at secondary school,' she said. 'People do start making new friends *and* acting differently.'

'But I don't like it,' I told her.

'Tough,' she said, smiling wryly. 'It's the way things are, Soph. Stuff changes as you get older. You've just got to get used to it.'

'I guess,' I mumbled.

Dumping my school bag I went upstairs. After changing out of my school uniform, I picked up the script of *The Lion, the Witch and the Wardrobe* that was lying on my desk and sat down on my bed with it.

I turned to the page where Lucy has her first lines and read through it. As the words entered my brain, I shut my eyes. It was like entering a different world. A world that felt certain, secure. I knew what

would happen in the play, I knew what I was supposed
to do.

I sighed. Why couldn't real life be as straight-
forward?

Chapter Twelve

Over the next two weeks things didn't get any better. Kelly kept on teasing Harriet, and Ally hung around with Eve more and more. All the two of them ever seemed to talk about was Matthew and Nathan.

'Sophie. You'll never guess what!' Ally came running up to meet me at the bus stop. 'Eve rang last night.' She dropped her voice to an excited hiss. 'She went out with Matthew again and he said Nathan really really likes me *and* that he's thinking of asking me out.'

'That's great,' I said, forcing a smile. I was feeling really tired. I hadn't been able to sleep much the night before. I'd been too wound up thinking about the dances. A fortnight might have passed but I still hadn't got any better at dancing and it was really getting me down. I'd tried talking to Harriet about it but she couldn't seem to see why I didn't just ask for help. 'It's stupid,' she kept saying. 'No one expects you to be perfect.'

But they did. She just didn't understand.

I definitely wasn't looking forward to the rehearsal

that night. How many times was I going to mess up this time?

'When do you think he's going to ask me out?' Ally said, her eyes excited. 'Maybe we could go on a double date with Eve and Matthew. It would be perfect!'

'Hi.' I looked round and saw Harriet walking towards us. I frowned. She looked different.

'Hi!' Ally exclaimed. 'You'll never guess what!'

As she relayed her news, I studied Harriet. What was it that was making her look different? 'Your trousers!' I exclaimed, interrupting Ally in mid-flow. 'You've got new trousers, Harriet.'

'And shoes,' Ally said, suddenly noticing too. 'They've got heels!'

Harriet looked embarrassed. 'I . . . er, got them yesterday after school – and the trousers.'

I stared. 'Why?'

'I just felt like it.' Harriet's cheeks started to go pink.

'You look really nice,' Ally said. She frowned. 'Have you got make-up on?'

'Just a bit of lip gloss and . . . um, a bit of mascara,' Harriet muttered.

Ally and I stared at her.

'It's no big deal,' she said quickly. 'Anyway, here's the bus. Come on!'

Ally and I exchanged looks and followed her to the

queue of people. No big deal? Who was Harriet trying to kid? She *never* wore make-up to school. And what was with the new trousers and shoes?

I had a horrible sinking feeling inside. I was sure I knew the answer. It had to be because of Kelly.

It was odd. Ally and I trying to persuade Harriet to dress like everyone else at the beginning of term was all right, but Harriet changing her clothes – and wearing make-up – because she was being picked on by Kelly was totally different.

'I know!' Ally exclaimed as we sat down. 'It's Ben, isn't it?' She looked as if she had just cracked some very puzzling code.

'Ben?' Harriet looked confused.

'He's the reason you're wearing make-up and have got new clothes, isn't he?' Ally said triumphantly. 'It's a quiz practice day.'

I could almost see the thoughts flying across Harriet's face. 'Yeah,' she said. 'That's right. It's because of Ben.'

But there was something in her eyes that just told me she was lying.

Ally grinned at her. 'Cool! So do you really thinks he likes you?'

'Well, he does talk to me quite a bit,' Harriet admitted. 'Last week he said he hopes we both make it on to the actual team. The team's being selected on Thursday.'

'So you got new trousers and shoes because of Ben?' I said disbelievingly.

'Yes.' Harriet avoided my eyes.

I continued to stare at her. 'So it doesn't have anything to do with K—'

Ally interrupted me. 'Maybe you should ask him out!'

Harriet turned in her seat so her back was to me. 'So do you really think Nathan might ask you out?'

That was it. Ally didn't need any more encouragement. For the rest of the journey she talked on and on about Nathan and how perfect they would be together. Harriet appeared to be listening intently but I knew she was just doing it so I wouldn't quiz her about the reasons behind her new clothes. I frowned at her. She didn't fool me that her clothes were for Ben. After all, if he *did* like her he wouldn't care what clothes she was wearing, and she knew it.

'Hey! Is this you?'

I was jerked out of my thoughts. A Year Ten girl had walked down the aisle and stopped by Harriet's and my seats. She was holding a newspaper and looking at me. I looked at the paper: there was a picture of me in the centre of the page and an article with the headline: *Film Star Sophie Does it Again!*

'Yes, it's me,' I admitted as Ally and Harriet looked round to see what was going on.

'It says you're going to be the lead in the Christmas show at the Palace Theatre.'

I nodded.

'Cool!' the girl said, looking impressed.

Other people had clearly seen the paper too. At least four people in my class had brought the paper in, including Mr Davey.

'Maybe we should organize a school trip to come and see you,' he smiled.

I sank down in my seat. Oh great. Just what I wanted: all my class coming to see me dance.

'So, how are the rehearsals going?' Mr Davey asked.

'Fine,' I mumbled.

'You're going to be out of school from next week, aren't you?' he said.

I nodded. In under a week's time the proper rehearsals with all the adults were starting.

'Has anyone got any questions they'd like to ask Sophie?' Mr Davey asked.

Lots of people stuck up their hands.

'Do you get paid?'

'How much time will you get off school?'

'Do you know loads of famous people?'

I answered the questions as best I could but I was very relieved when the bell finally went. At the moment, the last thing I felt like talking about was the play.

*

'And into positions, blue team!' Dizzy called that night. 'Let's see who's the best.'

Colette, Jack, Mark and I hurried forwards as Samantha's team – the red team – moved to the side. 'Come on,' Colette urged us, 'we can do it better than their team!'

The music blared out and we began the first half of the new dance we'd just been learning. That evening, just the principals had been called and Dizzy had come up with the idea of making us perform in our teams one after the other.

Luckily the dance wasn't too hard and I managed it with hardly a mistake.

'Well done,' Dizzy called as we finished. 'It's hard to choose between you but . . .' she paused, 'I think maybe the blue team were just slightly better.'

Jack and Mark exchanged high fives and Colette grinned at me in delight. At the side I could see Samantha scowling.

'Let's carry on and learn the rest of it,' Dizzy called. 'Come on, red team, come and join in.'

Samantha, Justine, David and Xav walked over. They stood in a group leaving a good couple of metres of space between them and us.

I glanced at Justine. She caught my eye but then looked away. She had hardly spoken to me since the day she had played the dance-sock trick. She just hung around with Samantha and the rest of her team and giggled with them whenever I made mistakes. But then there were times when I caught her looking almost lonely and it made me wonder if she was really happy with the way things were. I knew I wasn't. I hated the tension between the two teams. Memories of filming came back to me. It had been such good fun on the film set. No one had been competing with anyone else and nearly all of us had been friends. We'd played rounders together and hung out when we weren't filming. I wished my team and Justine's team could all just get on in the same way.

'OK,' Dizzy's voice interrupted my thoughts, 'and so from the finish on the spin you go forwards three steps and then Sophie and Justine you turn to the right like this.'

I copied Dizzy's movements as she spoke but I wasn't really concentrating. As I spun, Samantha stuck a foot out. I saw it too late.

'Oof!' I gasped as I tripped over and sprawled on the floor.

Dizzy stopped and looked round. 'What happened?'

'Nothing,' I said quickly, getting up. 'I just tripped.'

As Dizzy turned back to the front to carry on, I glared at Samantha. She smirked back at me.

And I wanted us all to get on? Yeah, like that was *really* going to happen.

*

At the end of the rehearsal, Dizzy made an announcement that made my blood run cold.

'As you all know, Claire, Stefan and I have to decide which of your two teams will perform on opening night. We need to do this fairly soon so Velda can draw up a performance schedule for the juveniles. So on Sunday we're going to spend the morning watching both teams. You'll have a chance to go through all the dances and the songs plus the scenes you have been doing with Claire. Afterwards we'll make our decision as to which team will be performing on opening night.'

Help! That meant I had just five days to be good enough to get my team chosen to perform on the opening night.

'We have got to be so good by Sunday!' Colette told me, Jack and Mark as we got our bags.

'Yeah,' Mark agreed. 'We've so got to be chosen.'

'How's the ballet coming on, Sophie?' Colette said. 'Have you been practising?'

I swallowed. 'I think I'm getting the hang of it now,' I lied.

'Good, I mean if you want me to practise with you, I can.'

'No, I'll be fine,' I said quickly.

I hoped I was right.

✹

Chapter Thirteen

'How do you think Harriet's doing?' I said anxiously on Thursday.

Ally was talking to Eve. She looked round distractedly. 'What?'

'Harriet. How do you think she's doing?'

It was the day of the quiz-team selection and Harriet, along with all the other people who wanted to be on the team, were spending their lunchtime doing a test quiz competition.

'She'll be doing fine,' Ally said.

I checked my watch. 'She should be back soon, shouldn't she?'

But Ally had already turned back to Eve and wasn't listening. 'So it starts at seven thirty?'

'Yes. Do you want to come round to mine first?' Eve replied. 'We could get ready together.'

'Definitely!' Ally told her.

I knew they were talking about a party they were going to at the weekend. Claire, one of the girls in their class, was having a proper party with boys. Ally was really looking forward to it because Nathan was going.

'I wonder what Harriet's doing now?' I said anxiously.

Ally shrugged. 'So what are you going to wear?' she said to Eve. 'I thought I might wear my short silver skirt – do you think Nathan will like it, though?'

A wave of irritation swept over me. Fair enough, the party was important, but Ally could at least seem a bit more interested in Harriet. She knew how much getting on to the quiz team meant to her.

'I hope she's done well,' I said. 'I hope she's got on the team. There's only four places.'

'Oh, stop stressing,' Ally said airily. She turned back to Eve. 'So what are you going to wear?'

I looked round in frustration and then I saw Harriet. 'Harriet!' I gasped, jumping off the wall.

She hurried towards us, her face split in a huge grin.

'Did you get in?' Ally demanded.

'Yes!' Harriet exclaimed. 'I'm in the team!'

'Well done,' Eve said.

'That's brilliant!' I said, hugging Harriet.

'I know!' she said. As I saw her beam, it struck me that I hadn't seen her looking so happy in a long time.

'What about Ben?' Ally asked. 'Did he get in?'

'He's the captain again,' Harriet said, nodding. 'Isn't it cool?'

'Definitely!' I said.

'Sophie was really stressing about it,' Ally said. 'But

I knew you'd get in. It's brilliant, Harriet. Well done.'

The bell rang.

'We'd better hurry,' Eve said to Ally. 'It's PE and you know what Miss Fraser is like if we're late.'

Ally nodded. 'I'll see you after school,' she said to Harriet and me.

'Bye,' we called as she and Eve hurried off.

'Lucky things,' I sighed. 'I wish we had PE not History.'

'Harriet!'

We looked round.

Ben was walking towards us. Harriet started to blush.

'I just wanted to say well done,' he said. 'You were great today. You really deserved to get on the team.'

'Thanks,' she smiled at him through her pinkness. 'You were really good too.'

'Hi, Ben.' Kelly came over to Ben. 'How are you?'

Couldn't Kelly get a hint? Ben was so not interested in her.

'Fine, thanks,' he said politely.

'Did you get into the quiz team?' Kelly asked.

Ben nodded.

'Cool!' Kelly smiled. 'I'll have to come and watch you in the competition.'

'Sure,' Ben said. 'The more supporters the better.' He glanced at Harriet. 'Harriet's in the team too,' he said warmly.

'Oh right,' Kelly said, sounding distinctly less impressed.

'Anyway, see you around,' Ben said. 'I'd better go.' He smiled at Harriet. 'Bye, Harriet. See you at the next practice.'

'Bye,' Harriet said, but her voice was quiet and I could see the happiness had vanished from her face.

Ben walked off.

Rachel and Leanne came over and Kelly turned to Harriet. 'So you're in the quiz team?'

Harriet nodded warily.

'That must mean you know the answers to loads of questions.' Kelly grinned. 'So what's a jock strap, then?' she asked.

'I-I don't know,' Harriet stammered, looking uncomfortable.

Kelly, Leanne and Rachel hooted with laughter.

I glared at them. 'Come on,' I said to Harriet.

'You really don't know what a jock strap is?' Kelly said incredulously.

'How about a wedgie?' Rachel said. 'Do you know what that is?'

They were making so much noise that people were looking at us now. Harriet blushed hotly. 'N-No.'

'But you're supposed to be brainy,' Kelly said. 'After all, you're on the quiz team.'

I'd had enough. 'Shut up, Kelly.'

'Or what?' Kelly turned on me. 'You think you're

really cool just because you've been in a film and you're in this stupid play thing. Well, no one's impressed, you know, Sophie.'

'Good,' I said, shrugging. 'I don't care what other people think.'

Kelly looked angry. 'You're such a bighead!'

'It's better than being a loser like you.' I looked at her scornfully. 'Get a life, Kelly. You're just pathetic!' I grabbed Harriet's arm. 'Come on, let's go.'

She seemed frozen with embarrassment. As I half dragged her away I saw her eyes brimming with humiliated tears. I pulled her into the nearest girls' toilets.

Luckily they were empty apart from a few Year Nine girls putting their make-up on. They glanced over but seeing that we were just Year Sevens ignored us.

'Are you OK?' I asked Harriet. Stupid question. I'd never seen her looking less OK in her life.

'Why do they have to be so mean?' Harriet said in a trembling voice.

'They're just idiots,' I said. 'You've got to ignore them.'

'But I can't.' A big tear plopped out of Harriet's eye and on to her cheek.

'You've got to,' I told her desperately. 'They won't stop unless you do.'

Harriet wiped her eyes with the back of her sleeve. I wished I knew what else to say.

The second bell rang. 'We should get to History,' I told her as the other girls left.

Harriet sniffed.

'Are you going to be all right?'

She nodded. 'Yeah,' she said, almost in a whisper and, biting her lip, she followed me to class.

Harriet hardly said a word for the rest of the day. She didn't answer a single question in History, usually one of her favourite subjects. She just stared at her desk looking miserable.

At going home time, she walked quickly to the cloakroom. I followed her, wishing I could cheer her up. 'I bet your dad's going to be pleased you got a place on the quiz team,' I said as we put our coats on.

She nodded but didn't say anything.

'So when's the first round of the competition?' I asked.

'The first week of December,' Harriet muttered.

Kelly came towards the cloakroom.

'I'm going to the loo,' Harriet said quickly, and she darted out of the cloakroom and into the girls' toilets opposite. I was about to follow her when I saw Ally coming down the corridor.

'Hi,' she said, bouncing over. 'Where's Harriet?'

'In the toilets,' I replied. I seized my chance. 'I need to talk to you about her. She's really ups—'

'Bye, Ally. See you on Saturday!' a girl from Ally's class interrupted.

'Yeah, see you, Michelle,' Ally called. She grinned at me. 'This party on Saturday's going to be cool! I'm going to get ready at Eve's house.'

'I know,' I said briefly. 'Look, Ally, I've got to talk to you. It's important.'

'Bye, Claire,' Ally called, waving to another friend over my shoulder. 'See you tomorrow! Sorry, what did you say?' she said distractedly to me.

'I've got to talk to you about Harriet –' I broke off. It was too late. Harriet was coming out of the toilets.

'Hi, Harriet!' Ally exclaimed. 'Shall we go and get the bus?'

'I'm not getting the bus today. I've got a dentist appointment and Dad's collecting me by the school gates,' Harriet replied. Her voice was flat but Ally didn't seem to notice. What a surprise. She was probably still thinking about the party.

'Come on, then, we'll walk with you to the gates,' Ally said. We started heading out of school. 'So I bet you can't wait until the quiz competition?'

Harriet shrugged.

Ally looked surprised. 'Are you OK?'

Harriet nodded. Ally smiled at her. 'Best of all it means you'll get to see even more of Ben.'

'No, I won't,' Harriet said flatly.

I looked at her. 'What do you mean?'

'I thought you said he was going to be captain,' Ally said.

'He is,' Harriet muttered.

'So, that means you'll see lots of him,' Ally said slowly as if Harriet was mad.

'No, I won't!' The words burst out of Harriet. 'Because I'm not going to be on the team.' She stared at us defiantly. 'I've decided I'm going to turn down my place.'

★

Chapter Fourteen

Ally and I stared at Harriet.

'What?' I gasped.

'But why?' Ally spluttered at almost the exact same time. 'You've been talking about getting on the team all term.'

'Well, I've changed my mind,' Harriet said.

'Is it because of Kelly and the others?' I asked quickly.

Harriet didn't answer.

'Harriet!' I exclaimed. 'You can't turn the quiz team down just because of some stupid comments.'

'What's Kelly been saying?' Ally demanded.

'I don't want to talk about it,' Harriet said sharply.

'This is stupid, Harriet,' I protested. 'You can't be serious.'

'I can and I am,' she said. 'Anyway it's not up to you, Sophie. It's my decision.'

'But . . .'

'I said it's my decision!' she exclaimed, her voice rising. A look of relief suddenly crossed her face. 'There's my dad.'

She half ran to the car, leaving Ally and I staring after her.

'Has she gone mad?' Ally exclaimed. 'What's up with her?'

Confusion and unhappiness surged through me and erupted in a flash of anger. 'Like you care!'

Ally stared at me. 'What's that supposed to mean?'

'I keep trying to talk to you about Harriet!' I exclaimed. 'I've been trying to tell you about her being bullied – but you're always too busy to listen. All you want to do is talk about Nathan or Eve. Sometimes I don't know if you even want to be friends with Harriet and me any more!'

Ally looked at me, open-mouthed. 'What? You think I don't want to be friends with you?'

'I don't know,' I said. 'Do you?'

Ally's eyes flashed angrily. 'If you even have to ask that question, Sophie, then I don't know if I do.'

'Fine!' I snapped. 'Then go off with your other friends. See if I care.'

'Right,' said Ally furiously. 'I will!' And she stormed off up the path to the bus stop.

My anger faded almost the second she marched away. What had I done? I hadn't meant to argue with her. I'd just been feeling upset and confused about Harriet. I started to run after her. 'Ally!' I called but she ignored me.

I hesitated and then slowed down. When Ally was

in a mood she was really in a mood and it was best to let her calm down in her own time. I trudged slowly to the bus stop feeling miserable. I hated arguing with her – and what about Harriet? Was she really going to turn the quiz team down? My head swirled. She couldn't; she'd wanted to get into the team so much and she'd been so happy. She couldn't turn it down just because of Kelly and the others.

When I reached the bus stop Ally turned her back on me, and when the bus arrived she pointedly sat down beside someone else.

I sighed and sat down near the front. I would deal with Ally another time. Right now, my thoughts were with Harriet.

By the time we reached Ashton I had decided that I would go round and see Harriet. I waited until I thought she would be back from the dentist and then headed over to her house.

'Hi, Sophie,' Mr Chase said, opening the door in an old T-shirt and jeans. 'Come to see Harriet?'

I nodded.

'Harriet,' Mr Chase called. 'Sophie's here!' He turned back to me. 'She's in her bedroom. Why don't you go on up.'

I hurried up the staircase just as Harriet opened her bedroom door. 'Sophie!' she said, looking surprised. 'What are you doing here?'

'I had to see you,' I said. 'Did you really mean what you said about the quiz team?'

Harriet's face tensed. 'Yes.'

'But why?' I said, going into her bedroom. 'You've been wanting to do it so much.'

'I don't want to talk about it,' Harriet said, walking over to her window and staring out.

'It's because of Kelly and the others, isn't it?' I said. I didn't wait for her to answer. 'Harriet, you can't turn down the quiz team because of them. They're not worth it. What does it matter what they think?'

Harriet whirled round. 'That's easy for you to say. You're not the one being picked on, Sophie!'

I was taken aback. Harriet never loses her temper. 'But . . .'

'Don't!' Harriet exclaimed furiously. 'Don't tell me to ignore them.'

I didn't know what to say.

'You don't know what it's like,' she went on. 'You can't possibly understand. How can you? You do everything right. You're popular. You know what to wear. People *like* you . . .'

'People like you too,' I interrupted.

'They call me a swot and teacher's pet!'

'Only Kelly and her friends,' I said. 'Harriet, this is dumb. You can't change yourself because of what they think. You've just got to be yourself.'

'Me? What about you?' Harriet cried.

'What?' I frowned.

'Think about it, Sophie,' she said. 'Are you really being yourself at your rehearsals? Why don't you just ask for help?'

I didn't have a clue what she was talking about. 'What are you going on about?' I said, frowning. 'Anyway,' I added quickly, 'it doesn't matter. This isn't about me. It's about you. You can't turn down the quiz team.'

'I can,' Harriet said.

'But . . .'

She put her hands over her ears. 'Look, just stay out of it. Leave me alone!'

There was a knock on the door. 'Is everything OK in there?' Mr Chase said. He sounded concerned. He wasn't the only one. I'd never seen Harriet look so mad. She was almost trembling with rage.

She strode to the door and opened it. 'Sophie's going,' she said.

Mr Chase looked very surprised. 'Oh, right.'

I looked at Harriet. Her face was rigid. 'Bye, Sophie.'

I didn't have much choice but to leave. 'Bye,' I muttered, and I hurried past Mr Chase down the stairs.

As Mr Chase followed me, Harriet shut her bedroom door with a bang.

'Is everything all right?' Mr Chase asked me as he

caught me up by the front door. 'Have you and Harriet had an argument?'

'Umm . . . sort of,' I replied.

'Oh well,' he said comfortingly, 'I'm sure you girls will make it up. See you soon, Sophie.'

I said goodbye and set off down their front path. As I reached the gateway, I saw Ally.

She stopped dead when she saw me.

I hesitated. There was no way I wanted another argument. Not now.

'What are you doing here?' Ally demanded.

'I came to see Harriet,' I replied. I hesitated. 'Is . . . is that why you're here?'

Ally nodded. There was a moment's pause and then suddenly Ally's face relaxed. 'Look, I'm sorry about earlier,' she blurted out.

'Me too.' The words rushed out of me in relief. 'I shouldn't have snapped at you. I know you care about Harriet.'

'Course I do,' Ally said. 'You two are my best friends.'

Warm and tingling feelings coursed through me. Deep down of course I knew it, but it was good to hear Ally say it.

'I don't know how you could ever have doubted it,' Ally said.

'Well, it's just that you've been spending so much time with Eve,' I said cautiously.

'Because we're in the same class,' Ally sighed. 'And I like her; she's really good fun to hang around with but that doesn't stop me being best friends with you and Harriet.' She frowned. 'You know, it's not been easy being in a different class from you two, seeing you go off to lessons together, hearing you talk about what you've been doing.'

I suddenly felt really awful. Poor Ally. I'd almost forgotten how hard it must have been for her. 'We never meant you to feel left out,' I said quickly.

'I know,' Ally said. 'And I didn't mean to make you feel that I wasn't bothered about you and Harriet any more. I am – I'm really bothered – but I've got to make new friends and Eve's nice.'

I nodded. I understood. 'She is.'

Ally smiled. 'So what's been going on with Harriet?' she asked.

'Let's go back to my house and talk about it,' I replied. 'I don't think there's any point in you trying to see Harriet now. She's really mad.'

'Harriet?' Ally said in surprise. 'But she never gets cross.'

'She never used to,' I corrected her. 'She's been acting really differently the last few weeks.'

'Because she's being picked on?' Ally said.

I nodded. 'Come on, let's go back to mine.'

On the way home, I told Ally everything that had been happening.

'I don't know what to do,' I finished.

Ally frowned. 'I had no idea they were picking on her so much. So that's why she got new trousers and shoes?'

'Yes,' I told her. 'And why she's stopped answering so many questions in class.' I sighed. 'We've got to make her see that she should just be herself. That it doesn't matter what people like Kelly think.'

As Ally nodded, I suddenly remembered what Harriet had said about me. She'd said I wasn't being myself. What had she been going on about? I pushed the thought to the back of my mind. It wasn't important. Right now what mattered was Harriet.

'What are we going to do?' Ally asked.

'I don't know,' I said. 'I guess we just leave it tonight and try talking to her tomorrow.'

But the next day, Harriet wouldn't speak to us at all. She sat with Emily on the bus and that's when I knew that she was really in a mood with us. Nothing on earth would normally persuade her to sit by her sister. And then in class she marched past me and went to an empty desk at the front of the room.

'Look who's got no friends,' Kelly teased.

Harriet blushed uncomfortably and looked at the desk top.

I went over to Harriet. 'Harriet, please can't we –'

'Go away,' she muttered, turning her back on me.

I hesitated.

'I mean it, Sophie. Go away.' Harriet looked up at me as if reading my mind. 'I'll move if you sit beside me.'

Giving up, I went back to my place. She really was mad.

For the rest of the day Harriet's bad mood continued.

'I'll try and talk to her tomorrow when we go riding,' Ally promised that evening as we got off the bus and watched Harriet unhappily march away.

'OK,' I sighed. I hated Harriet looking so miserable. 'Good luck.'

I found it was almost impossible to concentrate at the rehearsal the next day. Had Ally spoken to Harriet yet? Had she had made her see sense about the quiz team?

'Sophie!' Dizzy's sharp voice snapped me out of my brooding. 'Are you listening?'

'Er . . . yes,' I lied. Realizing everyone was looking at me, I felt my cheeks burn.

Dizzy frowned. 'OK, let's take that sequence from the top.'

The music started. I tried to follow the others but I got lost on the last few steps. I stopped in confusion.

Dizzy fixed me with a steely glare. 'So, you were listening were you, Sophie?'

I looked at the ground, willing it to open up and swallow me whole. 'No,' I muttered.

'Well, I'll go through it once more and this time maybe you'll do me the courtesy of paying attention.' Sarcasm positively dripped from Dizzy's voice.

With my face as red as a fire engine, I watched as she went through the steps and then I performed them – luckily to Dizzy's satisfaction.

'That's more like it,' she said briefly, and then she turned to address everyone. 'OK, guys, let's move on.'

As she showed us the next steps in the dance I caught Samantha grinning at me. I forced myself to focus on what Dizzy was saying. I couldn't afford to miss out bits of the dance again. Particularly not when there was just one day until the decision was going to be made as to which team was to perform on opening night. *My team*, I thought. *Oh please, let it be my team.*

'OK, everyone take a break apart from Sophie and Justine,' Dizzy called half an hour later. 'You two, I want to see you go through your solos.'

My heart plummeted. Oh no. Not the ballet. Justine and I walked over, avoiding each other's eyes as usual.

'Justine, you first,' Dizzy said.

I watched as Justine performed the dance. My spirits sank further. She looked perfect to me.

'Good,' Dizzy praised as she finished. 'Technically that's spot on, Justine.'

Justine flushed with pride.

However, as usual, Dizzy had criticism to follow the praise. 'Now you need to think a little more about character. Remember, Lucy isn't a trained ballet dancer. You need to try and evoke the feeling of a young girl dancing for sheer happiness. We need a real exuberance to shine through.'

Justine nodded.

Dizzy turned to me. 'OK, Sophie.'

I walked slowly out to the middle of the floor and took up the first position. As I waited for Dizzy to rewind the tape, I felt myself tensing. I had to be good. By tomorrow I had to perform this for Claire and Stefan. My stomach swirled like a washing machine. Dizzy pressed play and the music started.

I moved forwards but as I began the first spin I stumbled. Recovering, I tried to carry on but my body felt stiff and tense, and the harder I tried the worse I seemed to get. I could feel my face turning into one huge blush as I stumbled again.

Suddenly the music stopped. 'OK, stop there,' Dizzy said abruptly.

Straightening up, she walked over to me. All my muscles tensed. What was she going to say? I looked at the floor waiting for her to explode.

But when she spoke, her voice was soft. 'Sophie,

what's going on?' she said quietly. 'You can dance better than that.'

I looked at her.

'Well?' she said. 'Why are you making this dance into such a big deal?'

I didn't know what to say.

Dizzy frowned. 'OK, we'll leave it for now but I want to see you at the end of rehearsal today.' She clapped her hands. 'Right, guys, on your feet. Let's go through Aslan's dance.'

Everyone trooped on to the floor. I could feel people giving me curious looks but I kept my eyes on the ground.

'Ooh,' Samantha said mockingly as she passed me. 'See the teacher at the end of class. That can't be good.'

I ignored her but inside I was feeling sick to the pit of my stomach. What was Dizzy going to say to me? One thing was for sure, it wasn't going to be anything I wanted to hear.

To my relief, Dizzy kept us busy for the rest of the afternoon and everyone quickly forgot about the mess I'd made of the ballet solo.

Everyone, that is, apart from Samantha. 'Enjoy your talk with Dizzy,' she smirked as the rehearsal finished and everyone fetched their bags and coats.

I looked across the room to where Dizzy was talking

to Velda. Taking a deep breath, I slowly walked over. They were deep in discussion about the set. I hung around for a few moments but Dizzy didn't come over to me. Maybe she had forgotten about talking to me. A wild thought grabbed me. There was always tomorrow. Maybe if I practised really hard at home I could get the dance right and come in and surprise her. I began to back away. Guilt gnawed at me but I ignored it. Yes, I'd practise, that's what I'd do. I turned and hurried to the door.

✦

Chapter Fifteen

Mum was waiting in the foyer. 'I thought you were never coming out.' She smiled. 'I'd begun to think you'd been kept back for bad behaviour!'

Her joke was far too close to the truth for me to smile at it. I walked quickly out of the door.

'So how was today?' she asked as she followed me to the car.

'OK,' I muttered. I felt awful. I knew I should have stayed and spoken to Dizzy. She was going to be really mad with me. I almost wanted to turn back but I couldn't bring myself to.

I got into the car feeling sick. What was Dizzy going to say tomorrow? And it was the day the decision was going to be made. I groaned inwardly. Had I just totally messed everything up?

Mum started the car. 'It's amazing to think that you're starting proper rehearsals on Monday. The time seems to have flown by. It only seems a few weeks since you were auditioning.'

It seemed ages ago to me – a lifetime ago. Had I

once really been so delighted about doing the play?

'I can't believe the first performance is going to be in three weeks,' Mum went on. She looked at me. 'It's so exciting.'

I forced a smile and nodded.

'It's really wonderful to see you doing something like this,' Mum said. 'I know it's hard work but it's such a great experience.'

Suddenly I wanted to tell her everything. 'Mum . . .'

She didn't hear. 'As soon as you know which days you're going to be performing on I'm going to book tickets. I'm going to be so proud when I see you on that stage, Sophie. So very proud.'

The words I'd been going to say died on my tongue. I swallowed. How could I tell her how dreadful everything was now? How could I say that everything had all gone wrong?

Avoiding her eyes, I leant forwards and turned on the radio. As the music blasted out I leant back in my seat and looked out of the window. I didn't think I'd ever felt more alone in my whole life.

As soon as I got home I went up to my bedroom and, closing the door, threw myself on my bed. I was going to be a complete failure in the show. I was going to let my team down – let everyone down. Tears sprang to my eyes. No one in my family understood. There was nobody I could talk to. I thought about e-mailing Issy. At least she knew about acting and dancing, but my stomach shrank at the thought of telling her how useless I was. She was so confident and successful. What would she think of me when she found out I was such a failure?

I could talk to Harriet. As soon as the thought formed, I knew it was true but how *could* I pour my heart out to Harriet when she was still not speaking to me?

Oh this is stupid, I thought suddenly. Why are we arguing? We're best friends. So what if she wants to pull out of the quiz team because of what people think? It might be dumb but it's her choice.

I made up my mind. I was going to sort things out with her. We'd been friends too long to argue over whether she should be in the quiz team or not.

'Sophie! Ally's on the phone,' Mum called.

I hurried downstairs. Maybe Ally had managed to smooth things over with Harriet.

'Hi,' I said quickly, taking the phone from Mum. 'How did it go today?'

'Not well,' Ally admitted. 'She wouldn't talk about the quiz team at all and when I told her she was stupid to drop out she got in a real mood. She's not talking to me now, either. What are we going to do?'

'We're going to go round there and make up with her,' I said. 'I'm fed up with arguing. I want us all to be friends again and if that means accepting that she

159

isn't going to be on the quiz team then I guess that's what we've got to do.'

'It is?' Ally said uncertainly.

'It's better than arguing with her,' I told her. 'I'll meet you by the post office in five minutes. Let's go and sort this out.'

'OK,' Ally agreed.

Five minutes later we met up. 'What if she doesn't want to speak to us?' Ally said anxiously.

'We'll make her,' I said, feeling filled with determination. Everything else might be going wrong in my life, but my friendship with Harriet wasn't going to. 'Come on!' I marched to Harriet's house and rang the bell.

Harriet answered the door. As soon as she saw us she frowned. 'Go away!' she muttered. She tried to shut the door but I stepped into the doorway, stopping her.

'Harriet, wait,' I said. 'We're sorry. We shouldn't have tried to tell you what to do. It's up to you if you want to pull out of the quiz team.'

'Yeah,' Ally said. 'We don't want to argue with you any more. Can't we just be friends again?'

Harriet looked taken aback but then she nodded and her face relaxed. 'I don't want to argue with you either. Come in.'

We followed her up to her bedroom.

'I'm really sorry if I upset you the other day,' I said.

'It's OK,' she said, sitting down on her bed. 'I know you didn't mean to.' She sighed. 'It's just really hard having Kelly and the others making comments the whole time. I know they're just messing around and I shouldn't get upset but I do.' She looked at her knees.

Ally joined her on the bed and I sank down on to the beanbag by the bedside table.

'The more upset you get the more they're going to pick on you,' Ally advised her.

'I know.' Harriet rubbed her forehead. 'I hate secondary school.'

'It isn't that bad,' I said.

'It is,' Harriet told me. 'It's all about wearing the right things and about being cool enough.'

'It isn't,' I protested. 'I mean, OK, you have to try and fit in a bit if you don't want to get picked on, but it's not like you have to change what you're really like.'

'Sophie's right,' Ally said, backing me up. 'Yes, it helps to wear the right kind of clothes, but that's just on the outside; you don't have to change what you're like on the inside. You can still be you.' She smiled. 'You do look loads better with your new trousers and shoes.'

'They haven't stopped Kelly picking on me,' Harriet said with a sigh.

'She only picks on you because you react,' Ally commented. 'If you ignored her —'

'But it's so hard,' Harriet interrupted.

'It's not,' Ally told her. 'You've got to just tell yourself that it doesn't matter what she thinks.'

It was my turn to back Ally up. 'It's the only way to stop her. It doesn't matter how much you change yourself, she'll keep finding something to tease you about.' I took a deep breath. I didn't want to start an argument again but I had to say something about the quiz team. 'It's like the quiz team. You can turn it down but it won't stop her picking on you.'

'In fact it'll probably make her pick on you worse,' Ally said.

'So I might as well just do it?' Harriet said slowly.

Ally and I nodded.

'You'd be really good at it,' I said.

'And you'd really enjoy it,' Ally agreed.

'You know you love things like that,' I added. 'So trying to pretend you don't is pointless. I mean, how long are you going to pretend for? One year? Two years? All the way through school? If you go around pretending to be something you're not, you'll miss out on all the things you want to do.'

'I guess you're right,' Harriet admitted.

She actually seemed to be seeing sense! 'It's stupid trying to be something you're not just because of what other people expect,' I declared.

'It is,' Harriet agreed. She looked at me. 'So are you going to practise what you preach?'

'What?' I said, taken aback.

'Are you going to follow your own advice?'

'What are you talking about?' I asked.

'Sophie!' Harriet shook her head in disbelief. 'You keep going on about how stressful your rehearsals are. Have you stopped to think it's maybe because you're trying to be like other people want you to be?'

'I don't know what you mean,' I stammered.

'Well, from what you've said you seem to think that everyone expects you to be perfect,' Harriet went on. 'And you're trying to live up to that. Surely if you just admitted that you're not perfect at dancing and asked for help then the rehearsals might start getting better. You say I've been trying to fit in with what Kelly expects, but can't you see that you've sort of been doing the same thing?'

I stared at her. I wanted to argue but as her words sank into my brain I realized I couldn't. She was right. I had been trying so hard to live up to the image everyone had of me – Sophie the film star – that I'd been making myself miserable over the dancing. I wasn't a dancer. I should have just ignored what everyone might think and asked for as much extra help as Dizzy could give me right from the start. If I'd done that I might have actually been able to do the dances by now.

'Well?' Harriet said, looking at me.

'I guess you're right,' I said slowly. Reality began to sink in. 'I-I've been really dumb, haven't I?'

'I think we both have,' Harriet said softly.

Ally grinned at us. 'Well, what's new? Now me, of course, I never do anything stupid. But then I can't help being beautiful and popular and clever . . .'

Harriet glanced at me.

'Get her!' we both said at the same time.

I leapt off the beanbag – not the easiest thing in the world to do – and threw myself on to the bed. Together Harriet and I tickled Ally while she gasped and squealed.

'Get off!' she shrieked. 'I take it back. I said I take it back!'

At last Harriet and I relented. Giggling, we all sat up. Ally's hair was sticking up on end and she was pink in the face.

'You're looking very beautiful now, Ally,' I teased.

'Stunning,' Harriet put in.

'You're both idiots,' Ally said, but she was grinning.

Harriet got off the bed. 'Do you two want to stay for supper?' she said, looking much happier. 'I could ask Dad. We're having fish and chips.'

'Count me in,' I said. 'Can I ring my mum, though?'

Harriet nodded. 'Ally?'

Ally had gasped and jumped up, her hands over her mouth. 'I can't! It's Claire's party tonight. I'd almost forgotten. I've got to go. I'm supposed to be going round to Eve's to get ready.' She hurried to the door. 'I'd better go.'

'Good luck with Nathan!' I told her. 'Ring me in the morning before I go to rehearsal and tell me *everything*.'

'Remember, if you kiss him, we want to know,' Harriet said.

'All the details,' I reminded her.

Ally grinned. 'Keep your fingers crossed!'

I didn't sleep well that night. The portion of fish and chips I'd had at Harriet's house, plus the enormous tub of ice cream we'd demolished afterwards as we watched the video of *Scooby Doo*, seemed to sit like a boulder in my stomach. I tossed and turned, my mind whirling with thoughts.

How had Ally got on at the party? Had she and Nathan kissed? What was Dizzy going to say to me the next day? Something told me she wasn't going to be too pleased with me for disappearing after rehearsal without talking to her. What was I going to say to her? I needed to ask for her help. But if she was really mad with me . . .

And what about the rehearsal? The next day, Claire was going to decide which team would perform on the opening night. There was no way my dancing was good enough. My team weren't going to get chosen and it would be all my fault.

I finally fell asleep about three o'clock in the morning. When my alarm went at seven thirty I woke up feeling bleary-eyed. My head ached and all I wanted to do was crawl back under the covers and go back to sleep.

I didn't want to face Dizzy. I didn't want to go to the rehearsals. I was going to have to do my ballet solo in front of everyone. Oh no . . . My stomach did a loop the loop at the thought.

'Sophie!' Mum banged on my door. 'Are you awake? We need to leave in an hour.'

'I'm awake,' I said. 'Mum,' I called quickly before she could go downstairs. 'Could we go a bit earlier to rehearsals today?' I went to the door and opened it.

Mum was looking surprised. 'Go earlier? I thought the rehearsal didn't start until nine.'

'It doesn't, but I need to talk to Dizzy before the rehearsal starts,' I said. 'She's always there early.'

Mum shrugged. 'OK, we can go as soon as you want to. I'll go and get your packed lunch ready.' She set off down the stairs.

Closing my door, I quickly got dressed. I had to talk to Dizzy. I needed to ask for her help. I knew there was no way she could wave a magic wand and get me dancing perfectly by the rehearsal that morning.

But really, how much did that matter? Don't get me wrong. I wanted my team to be chosen for the first night, of course I did – but I could see that I had to be realistic. Surely what really mattered was that I could dance well enough when the show started. Maybe with Dizzy's help, I could improve sufficiently so that I didn't make a complete fool of myself when I was actually on the stage.

I was just about to leave the house when I remembered Ally. I checked my watch. Eight o'clock. She would kill me if I rang her so early. I'd have to call her when I got home that evening.

'Are you ready to go, then?' Mum said, picking up her car keys.

I took a deep breath. 'Yes, I'm ready,' I said.

When we reached Clawson Academy, I waved Mum off and then headed into the school. As I reached the foyer of the theatre, my feet slowed down. I felt sick. What was Dizzy going to say to me?

I walked nervously into the theatre. There was no one there. It all seemed very quiet. My heart beat quickly. When would Dizzy arrive? I felt like turning and running away. Maybe this was a bad idea. Maybe I should just wait until everyone arrived.

I heard the sound of voices. Velda and Dizzy. As they came into the theatre, my stomach lurched. Oh no, what was Dizzy going to say?

Dizzy stopped in surprise when she saw me. 'Sophie!'

'You're here early,' Velda said. 'Did you think the rehearsal started at half eight or something?'

'No, I, er . . . just wanted to see Dizzy,' I stammered. I looked at Dizzy. Her face had creased into a frown that looked seriously scary.

'Well, I'm glad you're here. I want a word with you. Why did you dash off like that last night?' she said, coming over to me. 'I told you I wanted to speak to you.'

'I-I'm sorry,' I said, hanging my head.

'This isn't a school play, Sophie,' Dizzy went on. 'It's a professional production. When you're asked to do something, you must do it. Disappearing like you did last night is not acceptable.'

I felt awful. 'I know. I should have stayed.'

'Yes,' Dizzy said seriously. 'You should have. I wanted to talk about your solo. I can't understand why you're finding it so difficult.'

'It's because I'm useless!' I exclaimed, the words spilling out of me. 'I've been trying to pretend I can dance but I can't. I get everything wrong. I can't do the solo. I can't do *any* of the dances!'

My outburst seemed to startle Dizzy. She put a hand on my arm and as she did, she looked into my face. 'Hey, calm down, Sophie. What's brought this on? What's all this about you being useless?'

'I am,' I said miserably. 'I should have asked for help but I thought people would think I was stupid, so I didn't. I keep making mistakes and getting things wrong.'

'But it's normal to make mistakes when you're learning a new dance,' Dizzy said. 'All the others get things wrong too.'

I looked at her. What did she mean? The others hardly ever seemed to get things wrong.

'You don't see it because you're dancing with them,' Dizzy went on. 'But they all make mistakes. Have you been really worried about this?'

I nodded. 'I thought I was the only one.'

'Oh, Sophie.' Dizzy shook her head. 'You should have said something to me. OK, so maybe you're not the quickest at picking up new dances but you're certainly not useless. The only dance you're really having problems with is your solo and I'm sure we can sort out your problems with that. But you've got to let me help you.' Her eyes bored into mine. 'And you've got to let me help you even when the others are watching. Do you understand?'

'Yes,' I said.

'Good.' Dizzy smiled. 'Go and get changed and we'll go through it before the others get here.'

It only took me two minutes to pull on my dance things and then I hurried back to Dizzy.

'We'll go through it from the beginning step by

step,' Dizzy said, 'just to make sure that it's clear in your mind.'

We started working slowly through the dance. We were just finishing the end sequence when the rest of the cast started to arrive.

'Good,' Dizzy said as I finished the last spin. 'And now I want you to dance the whole thing. I don't want you to worry if you make mistakes. I just want you to imagine you're Lucy. Show me her dancing for happiness, really believe that you're her.'

I glanced round. People were taking off their coats and looking at me curiously.

'Ignore everyone else,' Dizzy said softly. 'What they think doesn't matter. So you make some mistakes; I help you through them. It's nothing to do with anyone else. All that matters is that you get this dance right.'

I knew she was right. Trying to block out the rest of the cast, I took up my starting position.

'Try and imagine you're Lucy,' Dizzy said. 'In fact —' she paused as if she'd had a sudden idea — 'do you know the lines in this scene?'

I nodded.

'Well, let's go from about ten lines before the dance. I'll get my script and read Mr Tumnus's part.'

She fetched her script and a chair. 'OK, let's go from line twelve where Lucy says, "That was a lovely tea, Mr Tumnus."'

I thought for a moment and got the lines clear in my head, then I sat down on the chair – just like I would if I was Lucy – and I started. 'That was a lovely tea, Mr Tumnus.' As I said the lines I started to forget I was me and began to believe I was Lucy and I was really happy.

Suddenly the music began and I started to dance. It felt so much better. I didn't get everything right. I missed at least two turns but I remembered what Dizzy had said. A few mistakes didn't matter. I just had to really concentrate on being Lucy.

As I finished the final spin, Dizzy clapped. 'That was much better, Sophie. Well done!'

I glowed with pride and happiness. OK, it hadn't been perfect but I'd felt like I was dancing – really dancing. 'Take a quick break now,' Dizzy said. 'We'll be starting in five minutes. I'll just go and find out where Stefan and Claire are.'

I headed over to my bag, wishing I'd asked for help sooner. Maybe if I had, I'd have been able to do all the dances really well by now. I tried to remember what I'd thought that morning. Being chosen today to do the first performance wasn't really important. What mattered was being good enough by the time I got to perform on stage in three weeks' time – whether that was for the first performance or not.

I tried very hard to believe it.

'Sophie.'

I glanced round. It was Justine.

'You . . . you danced that solo really well,' she said.

She was being nice to me! Why? We'd hardly said a word to each other for the last three weeks. I stared at her warily.

The silence lengthened and a faint blush spread across her cheeks. 'I . . . er, better go.' She looked genuinely uncomfortable.

'Wait,' I said, as she turned. 'Thanks,' I told her.

I smiled tentatively and she smiled back.

'Justine!' Samantha came stalking over. 'What are you doing talking to *her*? Come on. Let's go and get our shoes on.'

Justine shot me an almost apologetic look and hurried off. I stared after her. Why had she come over to me? Had she really meant it when she said I'd danced well? I remembered the way she had smiled at me. It had seemed like a real smile. But then she *was* good at acting . . .

Oh, this was *stupid*. Suddenly I realized I was fed up with having to be suspicious, fed up with all the ignoring and staying on different sides of the room. I wanted to be friends. And not just Justine and me. I wanted everyone in the two teams to get on. I hated feeling we were always in a competition against each other.

'OK, guys,' Dizzy called. 'Time for a warm-up.'

After the warm-up Claire sat us down and explained that we were going to run through the play,

172

doing all the dances and songs and acting out the scenes that we had rehearsed with her.

'It'll give Dizzy, Stefan and I a chance to evaluate your progress so far,' she explained. 'And, of course, to choose the team that will be performing on the first night. Principals, you'll be acting alternate scenes for me, apart from the scene at Mr Tumnus's house. I want to see both Sophie and Justine do that. Justine first and then Sophie. OK.' She clapped her hands. 'We've got a lot to get through so let's have you into your positions for the first dance.'

As the rest of the cast started the first dance I saw Colette whispering something to Mark and Jack. She glanced over at me and, seeing me watching, beckoned me over.

'We've got a plan,' she hissed when I joined them. 'We're going to play a trick on Justine in the scene at Mr Tumnus's house. It should be funny.'

'And hopefully it will put her off so she makes a mess of the scene,' Mark said. 'She's not that great at remembering the lines from that scene anyway. It should make you look even better.'

'What are you going to do?' I asked, feeling worried. I wasn't sure I wanted them to play a trick on Justine now.

'Well, you know you have to sit down and have tea with Mr Tumnus?' Colette said.

'Yes,' I replied slowly. Part of the scene involved

Lucy sitting down and drinking a cup of tea and eating sandwiches with Mr Tumnus.

'And over the last few weeks you've been practising with real food?' Colette continued.

I nodded.

'Well, we thought we could change the food on the tea table to put Justine off. So we're going to swap the plain ham sandwiches you normally eat, for ham and –' she grinned at Jack and Mark – 'mustard sandwiches. Jack brought some for his lunch.'

'It's really strong mustard,' Jack put in. 'The type that makes your eyes water. We'll swap them back before you have to do the scene of course, Sophie.'

'It will be so funny to see Justine's face,' Colette giggled. 'She'll have to try and keep acting and she'll have a mouthful of mustard!'

'But that's mean!' I burst out. It was a horrible trick. 'Don't do it. Please. It's not fair.'

'Whose side are you on?' Colette said in surprise. 'Don't you want our team to look good?'

'Yeah, but not by making Justine eat mustard,' I protested.

'It's not that bad,' Jack said. 'It's not like we're poisoning her or anything.' He looked at the others. 'Come on, let's go and swap the food now while Velda's out of the theatre.'

'No!' I protested, but they took no notice.

Getting up, they went to Jack's bag and then to

the table at the side of the room where all the props were kept. They checked around. Dizzy, Stefan and Claire were all watching the dancing, and Justine's team were sitting in their usual huddle. No one saw them quickly remove the sandwiches Velda had made and swap them for Jack's extra-strong mustard ones.

I felt awful. Poor Justine – and she'd even tried to be nice to me that morning. I bit my fingernails. What could I do? I could swap them back but Colette and the others were bound to see me and try and stop me.

The dance finished and it was time for the first scene. I headed on to the stage. Worry jumped around inside me and then I remembered. There was one scene when Lucy was off stage for ages while her brothers and sisters were on stage. It was while they were playing hide-and-seek. Lucy had gone through the wardrobe into Narnia and they were looking for her. *Maybe I can get to the table then.* Yes, that's what I'd do.

'And five, six, seven, eight!' Dizzy counted us in for our first dance.

Forcing myself to concentrate, I pushed thoughts of Justine and the trick to the back of my mind. I'd deal with the sandwiches when I got a chance. Right now I needed to make a good impression.

The scenes went by in a whirl. As the time came for Colette, Jack and Mark to go on stage and act without me, I felt myself growing nervous. Could I swap the sandwiches? I had to!

But to my dismay, when the scene started Velda went over to the props table and started tidying things up on it. I couldn't go there now. If she saw what I was doing the whole trick would come out and Colette and the others would get into real trouble.

My skin prickled. What could I do?

Suddenly I saw Justine leave her group and go over to the drinks' table. Acting without thinking, I hurried over. OK, so maybe I couldn't swap the sandwiches but I could stop her eating them.

'Justine,' I said urgently. 'I need to talk to you.'

She must have seen the worry on my face because she frowned. 'What is it?' she said, sounding alarmed.

'You mustn't eat the sandwiches on the tea table.' I looked round. Colette and the others were busy in their scene and not watching me. 'They've got mustard in. It's a trick!'

I explained all about it. Justine's eyes widened. 'I hate mustard,' she whispered.

'Me too,' I said. 'That's why I wanted to tell you. I won't have a chance to swap them back but you should be able to. Just wait till Velda leaves the table. The normal sandwiches are on a plate at the side. Put some of them on top of the mustard sandwiches and only eat the ones you know are OK.'

She looked almost as if she couldn't believe it.

'Thanks.' She hesitated. 'But . . . but why have you told me, Sophie? I'd have thought you'd have wanted me to mess up the scene.'

I bit my lip. Did I really mean what I was going to say? Yes, I decided, yes, I did. 'I'm fed up with not being friends,' I admitted. 'I hate all the fighting between the two teams. And it's a mean trick and I'd hate it if it was played on me.'

Justine's eyes met mine. 'Thanks,' she said. 'And I don't want to fight any more either. I never really wanted to but it's Samantha. She just doesn't want any of us to have anything to do with your team. She really hates Colette and she's desperate for our team to be chosen for the first night to prove she's better than her.'

I looked round. I was going to be needed on stage any minute. 'Just because Colette and Samantha don't get on doesn't mean we have to hate each other too.' I heard Jack saying a line that was just before my entrance. 'I'd better go. Look, see you later.'

'Yeah, later,' Justine said. 'And Sophie – thanks.' She sounded like she meant it.

I hurried to the stage and just made my entrance in time.

When it came to the scene with Mr Tumnus I watched Justine with bated breath. I wasn't the only one. Colette, Mark and Jack were leaning forwards on their chairs, watching in anticipation. Their faces were a picture when Justine took a bite of a sandwich, then chewed it and swallowed it as normal. They looked totally shocked.

'She must like mustard!' Mark said.

'Her face didn't even flicker,' Jack exclaimed. 'That's some acting. I'd have been really thrown.'

Colette looked really disappointed. I kept as quiet as a very quiet mouse. I didn't think they'd be too pleased with me if they found out the truth.

Justine did the scene very well; she was perfect on the dance and everyone clapped when she finished. As I made my way to the stage to do the scene after her, butterflies flapped in my stomach. There was no way I would be as good. But I tried to remember what Dizzy had said. A few mistakes weren't important; all that mattered was that I looked like Lucy.

As the scene was reset, I watched Colette quickly swap the mustard sandwiches back for the normal ones when Velda wasn't looking. Luckily Colette didn't seem to notice that a few of the sandwiches had gone missing.

I think I did the scene OK. People clapped me, too, when I finished and I smiled all the way back to my seat. OK, I hadn't been as perfect as Justine but I was just relieved it was over and I hadn't made a total mess of it.

The rest of the morning flew by. I wondered which team would be chosen. My team seemed better at remembering their lines. I had a feeling I was acting well, but I still made some mistakes with the dances.

At last we were doing the final dance. We spun, held up our arms and it was over. We'd gone through the whole thing.

Claire, Dizzy and Stefan clapped as Dizzy turned off the music and we lowered our arms. I was out of breath and I had a stitch. I put my hands on my knees and drew in deep gulps of air. I wasn't the only one. Even the really good dancers looked slightly pink and sweaty.

'I'm exhausted!' Colette gasped beside me.

'Me too,' I agreed.

'Good work everyone,' Claire announced. 'You really have done very well to learn and remember so much.' She smiled. 'Now go and have a lunchbreak. You deserve it.'

'Back at one thirty!' Velda called, jotting down the time on her clipboard.

Colette's shoulders sagged. 'So we've got to wait until after lunch to hear which team's been picked.'

'I suppose they want to discuss it,' Jack said.

'We were better than the red team,' Colette said. 'They forgot more lines than we did.'

'But their dancing was good,' I put in.

'Well, there's no point worrying about it,' Mark said practically. 'We can't change things now. Let's go and have lunch.'

As I followed him over to our bags I found myself wishing I had asked Dizzy for help earlier. Maybe if I had, I could have really improved my dancing and given our team a much better chance.

Suddenly I didn't feel hungry any more. What if my team didn't get chosen because of me?

As I picked up my bag, Justine came over. 'Hi,' she said shyly. 'You were really good.'

'You too,' I replied. 'Your dancing was brilliant. You did the solo perfectly.'

'Thanks to you,' she smiled. 'If you hadn't told me about that mustard . . .' She broke off. Colette, who was standing nearby with Mark, was staring at me.

'You told her!' she exclaimed. 'Sophie, how could you?'

Oh no, Colette was really mad. 'I-I . . .' I broke off. Hang on, why was I trying to make excuses? I'd done the right thing. I frowned. 'I thought it was a mean trick,' I told her, putting my chin up. 'It wasn't fair.'

Colette gaped.

I glanced at Justine. She flashed me a quick smile and, emboldened, I went on. 'I don't want to fight with Justine any more,' I told Colette. 'It's stupid. So what if their team gets chosen to perform first? I don't care. I just want to be friends.'

'Me too,' Justine said, stepping forwards and standing beside me. 'When we were doing the film everyone got on and it was really fun. I want it to be like that here.'

Colette looked like she didn't know what to say.

'Sounds good to me,' Mark put in. I looked at him in surprise. He shrugged. 'I'm fed up with all this fighting too. OK, you and Samantha are never going to get on, Colette, but it doesn't mean the rest of us have to be sworn enemies. I quite like David and Xav.'

'Yeah, me too,' Jack said. 'And you've got nothing against Justine, have you, Colette? Apart from the fact she's in Samantha's team.'

Colette hesitated. 'No,' she admitted. 'I guess not.'

'So let's all just get on,' Jack said. He smiled at me. 'You did the right thing to tell Justine about the sandwiches, Soph.'

I smiled back at him.

'Well?' Mark said to Colette.

'OK,' she sighed. 'We can call a truce.' She frowned. 'Though I'm *not* being friends with Samantha.'

Mark grinned. 'I'm not expecting miracles to happen.'

I looked at Justine. 'Do you want to eat your lunch with us?'

She nodded. 'Yes, please.'

'I'll go and speak to David and Xav,' Mark said. 'You coming, Jack?'

They set off and Justine and I sat down together. We'd just opened our sandwiches when Samantha came over.

'What are you doing sitting with her?' she said to Justine.

I met her angry gaze. 'We're going to be friends,' I said.

'Yeah,' Justine said. 'We're fed up with arguing. Everyone is. Look.' She nodded to where Mark, Colette and Jack were laughing with David and Xav.

Samantha stared. 'But . . .'

'You might as well just accept it,' I told her. She might be fourteen but there was no way I was going to be intimidated by her any more. 'We're not changing our minds.'

'Justine!' Samantha appealed.

Justine shrugged. 'I'm with Sophie,' she said coolly.

Samantha glared at her and stalked off. For the rest of lunchtime she sat by herself.

At one thirty, Velda called to us that lunchbreak was over. 'Grab a chair and bring it into the middle,' she instructed. 'Claire, Dizzy and Stefan will be here in a moment.'

Realizing I needed to go to the toilet, I hurried out. I knew Claire didn't like people going out to the bathroom in between breaks. My heart pounding, I hurried into the cubicle. It was the big moment. We were finally about to find out which team had been chosen.

I was just coming back out of the toilets when I heard Claire's voice. She was walking down the stairs with Dizzy and Stefan. 'It's very difficult. Justine is clearly better at dancing than Sophie but in everything else . . .' Her voice trailed off. 'I hope we've made the right choice.'

I froze with my hand on the door. They were talking about the teams!

'I'm positive we have,' I heard Dizzy say. 'I know Sophie's had a few problems with the dancing but, like I've been saying, I'm really certain we've sorted those problems out now. She'll be ready by the time of the first performance. Trust me.'

'Well, if you're sure,' Claire said, and then their voices faded as they went into the theatre.

My head swirled. Had I heard right? It sounded like they had chosen *my* team. I wanted to race into the theatre straight away but I forced myself to wait a few moments in case they realized I'd been nearby and had overheard. By the time I slipped into the theatre, they were sitting down at three chairs Velda had put out for them.

I quickly sat down beside Justine.

'OK,' Claire said, looking round at us. 'In a moment I'll give you your notes on the performance this morning but first I want to let you know that we've decided which team will be performing on opening night. It was a difficult decision but . . .' she paused and then smiled, 'it will be the blue team, that's with the principals Sophie, Colette, Jack and Mark.'

The breath whooshed out of me and for a moment I felt giddy with relief.

'Yes!' Colette exclaimed.

Around us everyone clapped – everyone, that is, except Samantha. Justine smiled at me and mouthed *'Well done'*. David and Xav gave us the thumbs-up sign.

A warm glow spread through me. We'd done it, we'd really done it!

Jack banged me on the back and Colette hugged me. 'Isn't it brilliant, Soph!' she cried.

'Brilliant!' I agreed, feeling like I was going to faint with happiness.

'OK, everyone settle down,' Claire called.

As Claire started talking again, I glanced at Dizzy. I knew how much I had to thank her for. From what she'd been saying to Claire it was clear that she'd been arguing that my dancing would be good enough by the time of the performance.

It took Claire an hour to go through all her comments on our run-through that morning.

'Take five minutes,' she said when she finally finished. 'Then Stefan wants to go through some of the songs with you.'

As everyone got up and stretched I went over to Dizzy.

'Pleased your team's been chosen for the first night, then?' she said to me.

'Very,' I replied. 'Thank you for choosing us.'

'It was a joint decision. But you know you've still got some work to do before you get your dancing up to performance standard,' Dizzy said.

I nodded. 'I'm going to practise and practise.'

'Good.' Dizzy looked me in the eyes. 'Don't let me down, Sophie.'

'I won't,' I promised.

✦

Chapter Sixteen

As soon as I got home, I rang Ally to tell her my news but she wasn't there. 'Sorry, Sophie, she's at Harriet's house,' Ally's mum told me. 'Do you want me to take a message?'

'No, it's OK,' I said. 'I'll go round to Harriet's and see them both.'

They were in the garden cleaning out Pickles, Harriet's rabbit, when I arrived.

'Sophie!' Ally exclaimed, jumping to her feet and knocking the bag of hay all over the lawn. 'What happened at the rehearsal?'

'Did your team get chosen?' Harriet demanded.

I grinned. 'Yeah!'

They squealed and ran over to hug me.

'Well done!' Harriet cried.

'I knew you'd be OK!' Ally said.

'Only just,' I admitted, and I told them about Dizzy having to persuade Claire and Stefan that my dancing would be good enough by the opening night. 'I've promised her I'm going to practise loads. She was really kind. She said she'll help me with the dances.' I looked at Harriet. 'You were right. I have been worrying about what other people think of me and it's stupid. From now on I'm going to ask Dizzy for help whenever I need it. All I want is to be good enough by the time the show starts so that I don't let people down.'

Harriet beamed at me. 'That's brilliant, Sophie.' She hesitated. 'I've been thinking about things too and . . . well,' she took a nervous breath, 'I'm going to do the quiz team.'

My eyes widened in delight. 'Harriet, that's great!'

'What you said is so true.' She looked at me. 'Kelly will tease me whatever I decide, so I might as well just do it and enjoy it.'

'Cool!' Ally said.

'So what are you going to do about Kelly?' I asked Harriet.

'Try and ignore her.' Harriet frowned anxiously. 'I wish you weren't going to be at rehearsals, though. It's going to be weird not having you in school.'

I nodded. It was going to be weird for me too. From Monday onwards I was going to be rehearsing full time and, for the next three weeks, I'd be doing my schoolwork during breaks in rehearsal with a teacher from Clawson Academy. Once the play started I'd be back at school, although I'd have to leave at lunchtime on the days I was performing.

'I'll be back at school soon,' I said. 'And then it will be the Christmas holidays.'

'And you'll still have me to hang around with at breaktime,' Ally said to Harriet.

'Yeah,' Harriet said, but I could tell she was still dreading me not being there.

'We should have a sleepover next weekend,' I said. 'At my house on Saturday. Actually, no,' I said, suddenly remembering. 'Saturday's no good. I've got a radio interview about the play first thing on Sunday morning and then a rehearsal. I bet Mum won't let me have a sleepover the night before.' Mum was funny about things like that. 'How about the weekend after? I know we've got that Sunday off.'

Harriet nodded eagerly but Ally shook her head. 'I can't come then,' she said awkwardly. 'I've invited Eve over to my house to stay a week on Saturday.'

It would be weird but . . . 'Well, she can come too,' I offered. 'I mean she's your friend now, Ally. We should get to know her.'

'You wouldn't mind?' Ally said uncertainly, looking from me to Harriet.

We both shook our heads. 'Course not,' Harriet told her.

Ally grinned in delight. 'Cool! I'll ask her. She really likes you both, you know. She said so last night at the party.'

My eyes widened. How could I have forgotten? 'The

188

party!' I squealed. 'What happened? Nathan? Did you kiss?' I could hardly get the words out quick enough.

Ally shook her head. 'No. Almost. He was talking to me and was really close and suddenly, well, I realized I didn't like him that much any more.'

Harriet rolled her eyes and I could tell she'd already heard the story. 'It was his eyebrows, Sophie.'

'His eyebrows?' I echoed.

'They meet in the middle,' Ally said. 'I'd never really noticed before but he was leaning closer and saying how much he liked me and I thought he was going to kiss me and then I saw them. They were like a great big beetle or something.' She shivered. 'I couldn't kiss him after that. I like him as a friend still but, urgh, kiss him? No way!'

I pushed my hands through my hair. 'I can't believe you, Ally. You've been going on about how much you want to go out with him all term!'

Ally shrugged. 'Well, not any more. I told him I liked him as a mate and that was that. He was OK about it and we're still going to be friends.'

I sighed. I'd really thought she was going to kiss Nathan and that she'd be able to tell Harriet and me about it. Looked like we were going to have to wait a bit longer before one of us actually snogged a boy.

A grin pulled at the corners of Ally's mouth. 'There was this other boy there that I liked, though. He's called Luke and he's a friend of Claire's brother. He's in Year Eight. We talked a bit and he said he'd see me at school.' A dreamy look filled her eyes. 'I wouldn't say no if *he* tried to kiss me!'

Harriet and I exchanged grins. One thing was for sure, life was never going to be boring with Ally around!

You know the way people say that time flies when you're having fun? Well, the next two weeks seemed to go by at supersonic speed. Starting proper rehearsals was brilliant. The adults in the cast were really good fun. There was Maureen, an actress who used to have a part on *Eastenders*, who was playing the witch. She was really frightening on stage but really good fun off it; she always had sweets and she told us loads of stories about what the rest of the cast of *Eastenders* were like. Then there was Robin, a brilliant ballet dancer who was Mr Tumnus; Clive, who played Aslan, and was really tall – he usually played giants in Christmas pantos; and Darren, who was a children's TV presenter, was Mr Beaver. We started rehearsing at nine o'clock each day and when I wasn't needed in scenes I had to do schoolwork that my teachers from Charles Hope had set me.

It was very different from being in a film. And it wasn't just the fact I had to do schoolwork – the whole atmosphere was different. On a film set there were often just a few actors and loads of technicians, and you spent ages getting made up and waiting around for a scene to be ready. But in the rehearsal room there were just two technical people — Velda and the deputy stage manager called Lauren — but lots of actors. We rehearsed scene after scene really quickly and there was hardly any hanging around. If I wasn't acting or doing schoolwork, I was at a singing or dancing rehearsal. It was really good fun. Everyone got on brilliantly and there was loads of talking and joking. I was really pleased I'd made up with Justine, and even Samantha and Colette seemed slightly less frosty to each other.

I was trying really hard with my dancing. Justine was helping me and so was Colette. I was getting better but I still made mistakes and it was sometimes difficult to find time to practise. There was so much else going on and when I got home in the evening I was much too tired to start dancing. It was all I could do to collapse in front of the TV and then drag myself to bed. *I'll be fine by the first night*, I thought. But at the back of my mind there was the nagging thought, *What if I'm not?*

I hardly had time to think about school, although I did ring Harriet every night to see how she was getting on. She said Kelly and the others were still teasing her but she was trying to ignore it.

'I can't wait till tomorrow night,' she told me on the Friday night before our sleepover. 'It seems ages since I saw you. What are we going to do?'

'Mum said we can get a video and have a takeaway pizza,' I replied. 'Are Ally and Eve still all right to come?'

'Yeah,' Harriet answered. 'I think Eve's really looking forward to it.' I knew Harriet had been hanging around with Eve and Ally at breaktime.

'It'll be weird having her sleep over with us, though.' I frowned.

'It'll be good,' Harriet told me. 'She's really nice when you get to know her.'

'Yeah,' I said, but as I put the phone down I couldn't stop thinking about the sleepover. What was it going to be like with four of us? I couldn't imagine it. *Please*, I thought doubtfully, *please let it work out OK*.

I needn't have worried – the sleepover was just brilliant. Eve was really funny and I began to understand why Ally liked her so much. They had exactly the same silly sense of humour. First of all Eve started us off having a competition to see who could fit the most digestives in their mouth and then, just when Ally had her mouth stuffed full with three, Eve tickled her.

Ally burst out laughing, spraying digestives everywhere.

The rest of us all screamed and ducked the flying crumbs.

'Got you!' Eve grinned.

'Not fair!' Ally gasped and, picking up one of my

old beanie babies, a shaggy orang-utan, she hit Eve over the head. 'Take that!'

'Ow!' Eve squealed. She grabbed a lilac dolphin from my desk and began attacking Ally and the orang-utan with it. 'I'm Dilly the killer dolphin from the deep. Die, evil monkey, die!'

Harriet and I joined in and the next minute cuddly animals were flying around the room. By the time we stopped we were all red in the face and gasping with laughter.

'I need a drink,' I panted. 'Who wants a Coke?'

'Me!' three voices exclaimed.

As we headed on to the landing, Ally said, 'I'm going to go to the loo. I'll see you in a minute.' She went up to the bathroom door and tried the handle but it was locked.

'Oi! I'm in here!' Tom shouted through the door.

'Still!' I exclaimed, joining Ally. Tom had been in the bathroom three quarters of an hour ago when I'd tried to go to the toilet. 'What are you doing in there?' I demanded.

Tom didn't reply.

I gave up. 'Just use the toilet in Mum and Dad's room,' I told Ally. The rest of us trooped downstairs. 'And people say girls spend ages in the bathroom,' I commented.

'Maybe he's painting his nails,' Harriet giggled.

Jessica was in the lounge working on the computer.

'You mean to say Tom's *still* in the bathroom?' she said, looking up.

I nodded.

'He is *so* annoying.' Jessica frowned. 'He knows I want to wash my hair and he's been in there almost an hour.'

'What's he doing?' I said.

Jessica shook her head in exasperation. 'Probably trying out a new look for next Friday.'

'Next Friday?' I echoed, wondering what Tom was doing next weekend.

'It's his gig at the Junction,' Jessica informed me.

My eyes widened. Of course! I'd been so caught up with rehearsals and everything else I'd forgotten that Tom's band were about to perform at the Junction. I felt suddenly guilty. It was a really important night for him. 'Are you going to go and watch?' I asked Jess.

'Yeah,' she answered. 'So I'll give you all the goss'.'

I nodded. 'You'd better!' I carried on through into the kitchen with Eve and Harriet.

'You're so lucky, Sophie,' Eve said, sitting down at the kitchen table. 'Your family's so cool.'

Cool! Us? 'We're just normal.' I frowned.

'Normal?' Eve exclaimed. 'Your brother's in a band, your sister looks like a model, you've been in a film and now you're in a theatre show. That is *definitely* cool!'

I didn't know what to say. Maybe if it had been

someone else's family I would have thought the same but I certainly didn't feel that cool. I hurried to the fridge to hide my embarrassment. 'Coke?' I said, getting out a huge bottle.

Eve nodded. 'Yes, please.'

Harriet fetched some glasses. 'How's the play going anyway? We've all got tickets for the first night.'

'We managed to get seats together,' Eve said. 'They're near the front.'

'What are you talking about?' Ally asked, joining us.

'We were just telling Sophie we've all got tickets for the first night of her play,' Eve replied.

'Lots of other people from school are coming too,' Harriet added.

'Oh, great,' I groaned. 'Everyone can laugh at how useless my dancing is.'

Harriet frowned. 'But I thought you said your dancing was getting better.'

'It is,' I sighed. 'But I still make mistakes quite a lot of the time. And now there's just one week to go . . .'

'Arghhhhhhhhhhhhh!'

We all jumped as a muffled yell from upstairs interrupted me. It sounded like Tom.

Shooting a worried look at the others I dashed through to the lounge. 'Tom?' I called as they piled after me.

Jessica was standing up by the computer.

'Was that Tom?' I demanded.

She nodded. 'Yeah, I don't know what made him shout like . . .'

'ARGHHHHHHHHHH!' Tom appeared at the top of the staircase. He was wearing nothing but an old blue towel around his waist – but that wasn't what made my eyes widen.

'Your hair!' Jessica gasped.

My hands flew to my mouth. 'Your hair,' I echoed in a squeak.

Behind me, I heard my friends trying to stifle their giggles.

Tom looked down at us from the top of the staircase, an alarmed expression on his face. His hair, long enough now to reach just past his nose, was dripping with water.

It also happened to be the exact same colour as a tangerine!

✦

Chapter Seventeen

'What have you done?' Jessica gaped.

'I tried to dye my hair,' Tom said, coming down the stairs two at a time. He hurriedly hitched up his towel as he saw my friends. 'It was supposed to go blond, you know white-blond, like Chester Bennington or Eminem, but look!' He ran a hand through his unmistakably orange hair.

'Yeah, it doesn't exactly look like Eminem,' Jessica commented. A giggle burst out of her. 'More like Coco the clown!'

'Or Chris Evans!' Ally gasped.

That was it. A snort escaped me, and the next second, me, Jessica, Ally, Harriet and Eve were shrieking with laughter.

'I can't believe you've dyed your hair orange, Tom!' I exclaimed.

'It is just *so* sexy,' Jessica exploded with fresh peals of laughter. '*Not!*'

'Jess, help me!' Tom pleaded. 'I've got to get the dye out. It's the gig next Friday.' He groaned. 'Not to mention school.'

I caught Eve's eye. 'Still think my family are cool?'

She couldn't answer, she was laughing too much.

Tom glared at us. 'OK, don't help me, then.' He turned in what he seemed to imagine was a dignified way, and stalked back upstairs. Unfortunately for him the back of his hair was even worse than the front. He didn't seem to have put the dye on evenly and the back of his head was striped orange and bright yellow. At the sight of it we laughed even more helplessly.

Tom swung round. 'Some help you are,' he muttered bitterly.

Just then there was the sound of the back door opening. 'I'm home,' Mum called. Hearing our laughter, she came through to the lounge. 'What's going . . .' She saw Tom and her jaw dropped. 'Oh my goodness, Tom!' she exclaimed. 'What *have* you done?'

Mum was so not pleased with Tom for dyeing his hair, particularly when she found out that he'd also managed to get the dye – a permanent dye that didn't wash out – on to a bathroom towel, the bathmat, *and* the bathroom walls. However, once she had finished telling him off and he had promised to buy a new towel and bathmat with his savings from his job as a washer-up at the village pub, she was far more help than the rest of us had been. She sent him off to put some clothes on and then sat him down in the kitchen and gingerly examined his – very ginger – hair.

'Why did you do it?' she asked as we all sat round and grinned at him. 'It's a really . . . um . . . unusual colour.'

'I didn't mean it to turn out like this,' he groaned. 'Look, it was supposed to go white.' He held up the box the dye had come in. It showed a model – a girl – with white-blonde hair cut in a short spiky style.

'Yes, but if you look on the box,' Mum said, 'you can see it says that if you have very dark hair you need to apply a separate hair-lightener first. Then when it's gone lighter, you can dye it with this hair dye to make it go white. Didn't you read the instructions?'

'Yeah, but I just thought it was a scam to try and get you to buy two lots of dye. It cost me five pounds to get this one,' Tom said.

Mum shook her head. 'It's going to cost you a lot more to put it right. You're going to have to go to a proper hairdresser. It could cost up to fifty pounds.'

'Fifty pounds!' Tom said in dismay. 'But what about the amp I've been saving up for?' He looked at her hopefully. 'Couldn't you pay?'

'Definitely not,' Mum said, shaking her head. 'You got yourself into this mess, Tom, you can pay to get out of it. So what's it to be?' She fixed him with a look. 'Hair or new amp?'

Tom struggled for a moment. 'Hair,' he sighed at last.

Mum smiled. 'OK, I'll give my hairdresser a ring

and see when she can fit you in. She's very good at dyeing hair.'

'See if she can do it today, Mum,' Tom said.

Mum nodded, but when she got off the phone she said the soonest Helen the hairdresser could fit Tom in was Friday.

'You mean I've got to stay like this all a week?' Tom exclaimed, looking aghast.

'I'm afraid so,' Mum said. She paused. 'Though Helen did say she could fit you in first thing Monday morning for a haircut. If it's shorter it might not look quite so bad.'

'Cut my hair?' Tom's eyes widened in alarm. 'No way! I'm growing it.'

'I know, it's a shame,' Mum said. She sounded innocent but I could see the smile lurking at the corners of her mouth. 'But Helen did say that the dye might have damaged your hair and that you might have to cut most of the dye out on Friday anyway. Of course,' she added quickly, 'Dad and I don't mind paying for a haircut, Tom. So what do you say? Shall I book you in?'

Tom looked at Jessica and me. He looked like this was torture for him.

'You can't stay looking like that till next Friday,' Jessica said, glancing at his frizzy orange hair.

'And your hair looks much nicer short,' I put in. 'It really does.'

'Yeah,' Harriet agreed. 'I think so too.'

'Well?' Mum said to Tom.

He gave a deep sigh. 'OK,' he said, almost as if he was making a decision to have his leg cut off. 'I'll have it done.'

On Monday Tom and Mum set off for the hairdresser together first thing in the morning. 'Have fun!' I grinned as they left.

For once I'd been given a ten thirty call at rehearsal, which meant I had an hour to laze around the house before I had to get ready to go. Dad was working in the study and for a while I hung around in the kitchen in my pyjamas, eating toast and reading Jessica's latest copy of *Mizz*. However, after a bit I got bored and went to get dressed.

As I pulled on my jeans I thought about the play. It was hard to imagine that in a week's time it would have started and the first night would be over. We had three more days of rehearsal at Clawson Academy and then we were moving to the theatre. On Thursday and Friday there would be technical and dress rehearsals and then on Saturday it was the first night. Cold shivers ran down my spine. Just five days until I had to be perfect – not just getting by with only a few mistakes like I was at the moment. Absolutely spot-on, every-step-right perfect.

*

At ten o'clock, Mum arrived back to take me to rehearsal. 'So what does Tom's hair look like?' I asked as we drove into town.

'Better,' she replied. 'You don't notice the colour quite so much now it's short.'

'How short is it?' I asked curiously.

'Really very short, although he's had it left slightly long on top so he can spike it up or something for gigs and going out.' She smiled at me. 'Poor Tom. He was moaning about having to have his hair cut off all the way to school. He says he's going to grow it again.' She shook her head. 'Anyway, how are you feeling, love? I guess it's pretty nerve-racking being so close to opening night.'

I nodded.

Mum smiled. 'Don't worry, I'm sure you'll be fine.'

By mid-morning I was seriously doubting it. The rehearsal was fraught. Claire had decided we were going to have our first proper run-through, which meant going through the play from beginning to end instead of just working on one scene over and over again. It went badly, lots of people forgot their lines and Claire got increasingly tense.

'For goodness sake, guys, there are just five days until we open!' she shouted as Lauren, the deputy stage manager, had to prompt us for about the tenth time in the fifth scene. 'This isn't good enough!'

Everyone looked uncomfortable.

'Take five!' Claire snapped. 'And look through your lines.'

As Claire rattled off a list of instructions to Velda and Lauren, people sat down and silently got out their scripts. The usual jokey atmosphere had been replaced by an air of tension. I sat down next to Justine. She hadn't had much to do so far that day because Claire had decided that my team would act the first half and Justine's team would act the second half. I'd groaned when I heard because it meant that I would have to do the ballet solo. I was much better at it now but I still couldn't say I looked forward to it. I always went wrong at least once.

'It's not going well, is it?' Justine said to me in a low voice.

I shook my head. 'Claire's really stressed.'

'She's not the only one,' Justine said, nodding to where the adult actors were sitting. Some of them were walking up and down silently saying their lines, others were running their hands through their hair.

When Velda called us back on to the stage, all I could think about was the ballet solo.

Get it right, I thought as I went to stand ready to come on for the scene in Mr Tumnus's house. *Just get it right.*

I was thinking so hard about the dance that I almost

forgot my lines. At one point my mind seemed to go completely empty. What did I say next? Luckily the words came back to me just in time. I gasped them out. But it shook me and, after that, I gabbled and spoke too quickly.

Oh no, I was really messing things up. I saw Claire starting to frown.

Almost before I knew it, it was the solo. Determined to get it right, I tried too hard on the first spin and overbalanced. I stumbled my way through the rest of it. Claire's face grew darker by the second. She didn't stop me, though, and we carried on to the end of the first half.

I wasn't the only one to mess up; more lines were forgotten and entrances missed. By the time we had finished the run-through, Claire's head was in her hands.

'You know, I feel like walking out of here right now,' she told us as we all gathered nervously for the notes she was going to give us on our performance. 'In fact, why don't I just do that?' she said, her voice rising. 'We haven't got a show. That was a disgrace! You forgot your lines, you forgot the songs, you didn't know when you were coming on and you made mistakes in the dances.' She glared round at us all with her flashing lion-like eyes. 'Why?' she demanded. 'Just tell me why?'

I looked at the floor, feeling awful. I wasn't the only

one. All around me, people were crossing their arms and going red.

The silence lengthened and lengthened. At long last Claire sighed and sat back down. 'OK,' she said, sounding suddenly weary. 'Let's have the notes. I warn you, we may be here for some time.'

Claire was right. The notes took an hour and a half. She went through the play scene by scene telling us everything we had got wrong and everything she wanted to change. Afterwards we had lunch and then she made us run through each scene over and over again. We didn't finish until eight o'clock.

'I want you here at nine tomorrow morning,' she told us grimly. 'We're going to go through this play again and again until it's right.'

The next two days flew by. I'd never worked so hard in my life. When I wasn't acting I was dancing. I got up in the morning and practised, and before I went to bed at night I practised. I even dreamt about practising when I was asleep. But you know the most unfair thing of all? I didn't get any better. In fact, it began to seem like the more I concentrated and the harder I tried, the worse I got.

'Come on, Sophie,' Dizzy urged on Wednesday afternoon as I stumbled through a few steps. 'You were dancing better than this a week ago.'

I wanted to scream. How *could* I have been better a

week ago? And it wasn't just my dancing that was getting worse.

'Sophie,' Claire said, shaking her head after I'd acted out a scene. 'What's happened to you? That was nowhere near good enough. You were really tense and wooden. You have to be more natural.'

So my dancing was useless and now so was my acting. And it was just three days until the first performance . . . Great. Just great.

Harriet rang when I got home that night. 'How's it going?'

'Don't ask,' I sighed. 'It's a total nightmare. It's going to be a disaster — *I'm* going to be a disaster.'

'You won't,' Harriet said.

'Want to bet?' I said miserably. I swallowed and tried to think about something else. 'Anyway, how are you?'

'Good,' she said. 'I've been practising for the quiz competition. You are still coming, aren't you?'

Quiz night. Help! I'd forgotten all about it. It was on Friday evening after school. We were supposed to be having a dress rehearsal then but Claire hadn't told us which team would be needed for it yet. 'Um . . . I hope so,' I replied. 'But, well, I might not be able to.'

'Oh, Sophie!' Harriet exclaimed. 'I really want you to be there.'

'And I want to come,' I told her. 'But there's a

dress rehearsal that night and if I'm needed I'll have to go to that.'

Harriet was silent for a moment. 'OK,' she said at last. 'But try and come – please.'

'I will,' I promised. 'I really will.'

The next day it was the start of the technical rehearsal. It felt odd not going to Clawson Academy any more but going into the real theatre instead. I arrived at nine o'clock with the rest of the blue team. The red team had been called for three in the afternoon. We would go home then and they would stay until nine o'clock in the evening.

Backstage was a hive of activity. There seemed to be hundreds of people all dashing about, carrying costumes, hammering bits of scenery, carrying huge metal lights around and plugging in wires.

Velda was waiting by the stage to usher us all downstairs. 'Come on, quickly now. You must keep out of the stage crew's way.'

We went downstairs to the green room, and Velda explained what to expect. 'The technical rehearsal is a run-through for the technicians,' she told us, her voice strict. 'That's the lighting people, sound people, stage crew who move the scenery, and the stage management. The reason you're here is so that you can run through any bits of your scenes which have anything technical happening in them. There will be a lot of starting and stopping and waiting around and you're going to need to be very patient. Tempers will be short so if you don't want to be shouted at, do what you're asked when you're asked and otherwise keep out of the way.'

It sounded terrifying. I glanced around and was glad to see I wasn't the only one looking apprehensive.

Velda seemed to see our worried faces. 'Don't worry,' she said more kindly. 'I'm just warning you. Technical rehearsals are always difficult and it's best you're prepared. The technicians here are really good fun, but they've been working non-stop for three days and nights to get the set and lights and sound up and ready, so they're all tired and a bit grouchy. Once the show starts you'll see a different side to them. But for now, just do what you're asked and don't even think about complaining.' She pointed to a black box on the wall. 'Lauren will call through the tannoy system when you're needed,' she said. 'Otherwise just stay down here with Jackie and Rona.' She smiled at the two women from Clawson Academy who were going to be chaperoning us while we were in the theatre. 'And don't make too much noise. Now let me show you your dressing rooms.'

I never thought I would ever get bored with standing on a stage, but after six hours of hanging around, saying a few lines and then hanging around some more while the technicians hurried about or shouted to each other, I was more than ready to go home.

'Do you know which team is going to be needed for the dress rehearsal on Friday night?' I asked Velda on my way out.

'Claire hasn't said yet,' Velda said. 'But I think it will probably be your team. The plan is to have one dress rehearsal tomorrow afternoon about three o'clock and one tomorrow evening. I'd imagine Claire will want your team to do tomorrow evening, seeing as you'll be doing the first night. However, it will depend a bit on how the technical rehearsal goes. If we over-run then, the plans might need to be changed. I'll let you know tomorrow morning.'

'Thanks,' I said, my heart sinking. I wanted to go to the quiz competition and support Harriet but the chance of that looked to be very small indeed.

However, the next morning, when I arrived at the theatre, I was greeted with good news. Well, good for me anyway. The stage crew had had problems with some of the scenery the night before, which meant that the technical rehearsal was running way behind schedule. It now looked as if the dress rehearsals weren't going to take place until the next day.

'It's going to be very difficult,' Velda told us. 'We'll be very pushed for time but we'll have one dress rehearsal in the morning, that will be with the red team, and then one in the afternoon with the blue team.'

'But the show's tomorrow night,' Mark said.

'Yes. Like I say, we're going to be pushed for time. You'll only have a couple of hours or so between the dress rehearsal finishing and the first performance starting – but then it's going to be the same when you're doing a matinee and evening performance.'

'So what about today?' I asked. 'What are we doing?'

'The same as yesterday,' Velda said. 'You'll be here until three and then the red team will come and take over.'

'So that means we won't get a chance to have a proper rehearsal today?' a girl in the chorus, called Tania, asked.

'I'm afraid not,' Velda replied. 'It'll just be more starting and stopping.'

'So we've only really got the dress rehearsal left,' Colette said.

As Velda nodded, the delight I'd been feeling at being able to get to the quiz competition faded abruptly. No more practising, just the dress rehearsal! But . . . but . . . but I wasn't good enough. Images of the last dreadful rehearsal on Wednesday came back to me. *Help*, I thought, suddenly feeling as quivery as a pile of jelly. *What am I going to do?*

*

Dizzy did find time when the crew went to the pub for lunch to let us practise the dances on the stage. But my mind seemed to be switched on to panic mode and I made loads of mistakes.

'Sophie, come on!' Dizzy shouted as I went into a spin a couple of beats too late. 'Keep up!'

And step, two, three and forwards. The instructions pounded around in my head. I felt stiff and tense. *Oh, no*, I thought as I missed a lunge to the side, *Dizzy's going to kill me.*

But she didn't. Afterwards she just looked at me and shook her head. 'I'm not going to say anything, Sophie. I just hope you don't perform like that tomorrow night.'

I almost wished she had had a go at me. The disappointment in her gaze was horrible.

I bit my lip and looked down. *Oh, please*, I prayed desperately. *Please let me be OK tomorrow night!*

✦

Chapter Eighteen

'We'd better win,' Ally said to me and Eve as we found three seats near the front of our school hall.

It was a huge relief to be at the quiz competition that night, and to be able to think of something apart from the play. I looked at the stage. Four teams from four different schools were sitting there. Harriet was with Ben, a Year Eight girl called Anna and a Year Seven boy called Nikhil. She saw us and waved. We all waved back.

Good luck, I mouthed at her.

She smiled nervously.

Ally sat down and sighed. 'I can't believe it's a Friday night and we're back at school. We could be at the Junction tonight hearing Tom and his band play.'

'We'd never have got in, and anyway,' I looked at her sternly, 'you know you'd rather be here support-ing Harriet.'

Ally looked like she was actually giving it serious thought. 'Well . . .' she mused. She grinned at my outraged expression. 'I'm just joking. Of course I'd rather be here. Even if we could have got in at the Junction, I wouldn't have gone. This is Harriet's big night.'

I smiled at her.

'So, has Tom sorted out his hair?' Eve asked as we settled down.

'Yeah, he went to the hairdresser again today,' I told her.

'What did she do to his hair?' Ally asked.

'She dyed it dark brown again but she also gave him this red spray-on colour to use. It washes in and washes out. He gelled it up tonight into spikes for the gig and he coloured the end of each spike red.'

'That sounds cool,' Ally said.

I nodded. It had actually looked really good. 'Yeah,' I started to say but just then something – or rather someone – caught my eye. 'Look, Kelly's here!'

'And Leanne and Rachel,' Eve pointed out.

'I bet Kelly's come to try and ask Ben out again,' I said. 'I don't know why she doesn't just give up.'

Kelly, Leanne and Rachel sat a few rows away from us. They kept giggling and waving at Ben. He smiled briefly but then ignored them.

After about ten minutes the quiz began. Mr Johnson, our deputy head, was the quiz master. Sitting at a desk he read out the questions. If the contestants thought they knew the answers they had to press a buzzer which made a light in front of them light up. If they got the answer right then their team got to answer three questions as a team.

I'd thought it was going to be boring – I mean, quizzes about stuff like science and history and geography aren't my idea of fun – but it was actually exciting. The four teams were all really good. They kept pressing their buzzers halfway through the questions and Mr Johnson hardly gave them time to think.

Harriet was brilliant. She looked a bit nervous to start with but as soon as she had answered a few questions correctly she really got into it. In fact, she and Ben seemed to be competing for who could press their buzzer the quickest.

Gradually it became clear that the competition was going to be won by either our school or the team from St Mary's.

'Just one minute left,' Mr Johnson announced, glancing at the clock on the wall. 'And Charles Hope and St Mary's are joint leaders with two hundred points each, so for ten points and a chance of three bonus questions . . .' He paused before reading the question and I saw the members of both teams glance nervously at each other. This could be the deciding question.

I leant forwards. Could our team do it? *Come on*, I thought, *come on!*

Mr Johnson looked around. 'Who was the first Tudor king of . . .'

He hadn't even got the fifth word out before Harriet's buzzer went off.

'Harriet, Charles Hope!' Mr Johnson called.

'Henry the Seventh,' Harriet answered quickly.

'Correct. The first Tudor king of England was Henry the Seventh,' Mr Johnson said.

'Yes!' I saw Ben exclaim, clenching his fists. Harriet grinned at him in delight.

The people in the audience who were supporting Charles Hope clapped and cheered.

'Your three bonus questions start now,' Mr Johnson said. 'Who was Henry the Eighth's first wife?'

'Catherine of Aragon,' Ben called out.

Mr Johnson nodded.

'Who was on the throne before Elizabeth the First?'

'Mary the First,' Harriet answered.

Mr Johnson nodded again. 'And which king was responsible for the dissolution of the monasteries?'

There was a pause. 'I'm going to have to rush you,' Mr Johnson said, as Harriet, Ben, Anna and Nikhil quickly conferred. He waited about five seconds.

'Sorry, your time is . . .'

'Henry the Eighth!' Harriet burst out quickly.

'Correct!' Mr Johnson exclaimed. 'And now on with the next starter question. In which country is the city of . . .'

There was a loud buzzing noise. The time had run out.

'We've won!' I gasped.

'And the winners of the first round of the inter-school under-fourteen quiz are Charles Hope!' Mr Johnson announced, looking very pleased.

The applause was deafening. On stage, Harriet, Ben, Nikhil and Anna all jumped up in delight. Anna banged Nikhil on the back and then Ben hugged Harriet. She threw her arms round his neck.

'Look!' I squeaked to Ally.

Harriet and Ben both suddenly seemed to realize they were hugging. Looking very flustered, Harriet quickly stepped back. The next second, Anna and Nikhil were beside them, shouting in excitement.

'They hugged!' Ally said to me.

'I saw!' I said. Excitement raced through me. Hugging *had* to be a good sign.

The four teams all shook hands and then they came off the stage to be surrounded by their supporters.

Eve, Ally and I pushed our way through the crowds to meet Harriet. 'You were brilliant!' I cried as I reached her.

'Fantastic!' Ally agreed.

Harriet's eyes shone. 'It was such good fun!'

'You got loads of questions right,' Eve said. 'There's no way we'd have won without you.'

'Ben answered lots too,' Harriet said, glancing in Ben's direction. He was with a crowd of friends, standing near the table where drinks were being sold. He saw her looking and smiled.

'He likes you,' Eve said. 'It's totally obvious.'

Excitement seemed to bubble through Harriet. 'He's wonderful,' she sighed. She looked in Ben's direction again. He glanced at her at exactly the same time.

'I'm . . . I'm going to get a drink,' Harriet said, going red.

'We'll come with . . .' Ally broke off with a gasp as I trod on her foot — hard.

'We'll wait here,' I said quickly to Harriet.

'OK,' she replied.

'Ow! What was that for?' Ally demanded as Harriet made her way towards the drinks' table.

'Ben's over there,' I hissed. 'Maybe he'll go and talk to her.'

We watched as Harriet pushed her way through the crowd. Ben saw her too and headed after her.

'Look!' Eve exclaimed as he caught up with Harriet. He took her arm and said something. She hesitated and then nodded, and they swerved away from the drinks' table, stopping when they were in a quiet corner away from the crowd.

We watched agog as Ben leaned forwards. He seemed to be asking Harriet something. I saw her eyes widen and for a moment she didn't seem to know what to say. But then she nodded.

A grin broke out on Ben's face and, stepping forwards . . . he *KISSED* her.

'Ohmigod!' Ally squealed.

'They're kissing!' I gasped, my head going all swirly. Harriet had kissed a boy! She *was* kissing a boy! A real, lips-and-everything, proper kiss.

'Mr Johnson's going to kill them if he sees!' Eve said.

But it wasn't Mr Johnson Harriet had to worry about. Suddenly I realized that Kelly was watching them from the drinks' table. A furious look crossed her face and she started to march in Ben and Harriet's direction. Not stopping to think, I started pushing through the crowd. I had to get to Harriet first. There was no way I was going to let Kelly upset her on such a perfect day.

Just as I got close, I saw Ben smile at Harriet. 'I'll go and get you that drink, then?' I heard him say.

Harriet nodded and he headed off.

'Harriet!' I exclaimed.

Harriet turned. 'Sophie!' She looked like she had a light bulb shining inside her. 'Did you see?' she gasped. 'Ben kissed me. He's asked me out! He . . .' Her words dried up and her smile suddenly faded as she stared at someone over my shoulder.

I didn't have to look round to know who it was.

'So, you've got a boyfriend now, have you, Harriet?' Kelly's voice sneered. 'Think you're cool, do you? Well, you're just a pathetic geek and there's no way Ben will go out with you for long and . . .'

I turned, hot anger racing through me.

But before I could open my mouth, Harriet spoke. 'Get lost, Kelly!'

I swung round in astonishment.

'What?' Kelly exclaimed, sounding as stunned as I felt.

'You heard,' Harriet said, drawing herself up to her full height. 'Just get lost!'

Kelly gaped.

'You're the pathetic one, Kelly,' Harriet rushed on. 'Acting as if you're something special, expecting everyone to want to be the same as you.'

For once Kelly looked lost for words. 'L-L-Loser,' she managed to stammer.

'You can call me what you like.' Harriet shrugged, triumph flashing in her eyes. 'Cos you know what? I really don't care.'

At that moment Ben came back, carrying two cans of Coke. 'Hi, Kelly,' he said briefly. He gave Harriet one of the cans. 'Here,' he said, taking her hand.

It seemed to be the last straw for Kelly. Looking like she was about to explode with fury she stomped off.

Ben stared after her in surprise. 'What's up with her?'

'Nothing,' Harriet said. She smiled shyly at Ben. 'Thanks for the drink.'

Ben smiled back. 'That's OK.' Their eyes met and I felt my heart swell.

Wow. Could things get any better?

The rest of the evening passed in a blur. Kelly left almost immediately. I grinned as I watched her flounce out of the hall with Leanne and Rachel. Something told me she wouldn't be bothering Harriet much any more. Ben hardly left Harriet's side and she had a constant smile on her face. It was brilliant seeing her look so happy. When Dad arrived to collect me I managed to drag her away from Ben for a few minutes.

'I've got to go but I want all the details tomorrow,' I told her.

'What, *all* the details?' she teased.

'Yes, *all* the details,' I said meaningfully.

She grinned. 'OK. I'll see you after the play. Good luck.'

'Thanks.' My stomach did a double flip. 'I think I'm going to need it.'

Mum made me go to bed as soon as I got home but I couldn't sleep. At half eleven, I heard Jessica come home from the Junction.

Hearing her coming up the stairs, I went to my bedroom door. 'Hi.'

'Still awake?' she said, yawning. 'How did the quiz go?'

'Great – we won. What was the Junction like?' I asked eagerly. 'How was Tom's band?'

'They were really good,' Jess enthused. 'Everyone liked them. I'm sure they'll be asked to play again.'

'Brilliant,' I said, really pleased for Tom.

'Tom's still there celebrating,' Jessica went on. She shook her head. 'You should've seen him, Soph. He was like a rock star. He had all these girls hanging around him afterwards.' She grinned wickedly. 'Zak wasn't too pleased, as you can imagine.'

I grinned back. 'Good.' Zak was the arrogant lead singer who Jessica had had a thing with in the summer. He was the biggest poser ever.

'You know, I reckon he'll be going straight to the hairdresser tomorrow, having his hair cut like Tom's,' Jessica said. 'In fact, I bet Nick, Raj and Olly all do. Tom looked the coolest of them by far.'

My brother. A cool rock star. Wow! Maybe Ally's dream of him being on *Top of the Pops* wasn't so far-fetched after all.

Jess yawned again. 'Anyway, I'm knackered,' she said, heading towards her room. 'I'm going to bed.'

'Yeah,' I said, sighing. 'I suppose I should try and go to sleep too.'

Jessica paused. 'Don't worry about tomorrow,' she said. 'You'll be great, Sophie.'

'Yeah, right,' I muttered.

To my surprise, Jessica came over and hugged me. 'You will be,' she said softly. 'You always are.'

'Thanks,' I mumbled.

Feeling comforted but not convinced, I went back to bed.

By the time I arrived at the theatre for my dress rehearsal the next day I was so nervous, and my legs were wobbling so much as I walked, that I thought I was going to fall over.

'Good luck,' Mum said, giving me a hug at stage door. 'We'll all be in the audience cheering you on.' She kissed me. 'See you later.'

Suddenly I knew just how all those kings and queens who got beheaded felt as they walked up to the beheading block. As I walked slowly into the theatre, my stomach felt like it had butterflies the size of elephants flapping inside it. I was going to be sick. I just knew I was going to be sick.

To my surprise, the theatre was very quiet. The crew must have gone on a lunchbreak. The scenery was all set out for scene one. There was no one around. I hesitated and then walked on to the stage.

The auditorium was deserted, the chair seats all folded up. I looked around – at the high ceiling with its faded gold decorations, at the modern black lighting box at the back, at the red-curtained entrances. It was weird. For the last two days the place had been a bustle of activity and now it seemed so quiet and still. The air had an almost expectant feel as if it was waiting for something to happen. A shiver ran over my skin as I realized how old the theatre was. How many people had stood on this stage? How many plays had there been?

I took a deep breath of the people- and scenery-scented air, and felt a flicker of happiness ignite deep inside my stomach. It grew inside me, the flicker becoming a burning flame until it swept over me and knowledge exploded like a shower of fireworks into my brain. This was where I belonged. On a stage. In a theatre. Somewhere where I could act.

Suddenly my nerves dissolved. I wasn't scared of doing the play. I was excited – more excited than I had ever been in my life.

A grin spread across my face and I turned and ran off the stage, down the steps and into the green room.

'What's the hurry?' Velda said in surprise as I barged through the door.

'It's the dress rehearsal!' I exclaimed, feeling like every cell of my body was alight. Ignoring Velda's startled expression, I spun round. 'Isn't it great?'

My excitement didn't last for long enough. As I got ready, my nerves began slowly, but relentlessly, to creep back. By the time I was waiting in the darkness of the wings with everyone else for the play to start, my heart was thumping and my palms were sweaty. What if I went wrong in the dances? What if I fell over?

I nervously wiped my hands on the skirt of my dress. The orchestra began to play the overture — a three-minute mixture of all the songs that were in the show. My heart jumped into my throat. This was it. We were about to start.

I felt a hand on my shoulder and turned. It was Dizzy. 'Stay relaxed, Sophie,' she said softly. 'Don't worry about getting the dances right. Just go on that stage and be Lucy.' Her eyes stared into mine. 'Do you understand? Don't act — just be.'

I nodded slowly. *Just be.* Dizzy's words made sense. When I was acting well I never felt like I was acting; I felt like I became the person I was pretending to be.

'Go for it,' Dizzy smiled. 'I'll see you afterwards.'

She slipped away. The music changed. The heavy red curtains started to open and then the opening dance began.

It went perfectly but I hardly had time to whisper *well done* as the chorus ran off the stage before I was on.

The lights hit me. Colette, Jack and Mark were there and suddenly, standing on the stage again, looking at them in costume, I forgot about trying hard. I forgot about acting. I did what Dizzy had said and I became Lucy.

The lines sprang to my lips as if they had always

been in my head and, even more amazingly, so did the steps of the dance. By the time of Aslan's death scene, one of the biggest scenes at the end of the play, I was lost in another world. As I laid my head against the thick mane of Clive's costume, I felt real tears stinging my eyes.

'Oh, Aslan, don't be dead,' I sobbed. 'Please, please don't be dead!'

I could see tears on Colette's cheeks, too, as we held hands and sang for the loss of our brave dead friend.

As our voices rose together I was vaguely aware of people sniffing in the darkness of the auditorium.

Scene followed scene until suddenly we were singing the final jubilant song. On the last notes, the curtains closed. There was a pause and then they opened again to the sound of people clapping. For a moment I wondered whether we were going to go into the routine of bows that we had rehearsed the day before, but then the lights came up on the auditorium. I could see Dizzy and Claire and quite a few of the stage crew and front-of-house people from the theatre standing on their feet and clapping.

The next minute Claire was hurrying on to the stage. 'That,' she exclaimed, her eyes shining, 'was fantastic!'

I exchanged delighted looks with Colette, who was standing next to me.

'It was absolutely amazing,' Claire said. She strode over to me. 'Sophie, you were perfect!' she said, hugging me.

I was perfect! I felt like I was going to explode with delight.

'In fact,' she said, her eyes sweeping round the stage, 'everyone was great!' Her smile broadened as we all exchanged delighted looks. 'Now, all you've got to do is be that good tonight!'

The time between the dress rehearsal and the evening performance raced past. Costumes were whisked off us for cleaning and ironing, and the stage was quickly reset. As the stage crew raced around, all dressed in black clothes, the cast wandered about in dressing gowns, eating tea and redoing their make-up. Good luck cards and bouquets of flowers started being delivered from stage door. I was astonished when one of the bouquets was for me.

I read the card tied to the pink, purple and blue flowers: *To Sophie, our shining star. Remember we'll always love you. Hugs and kisses, Mum, Dad, Jessica and Tom.*

I had to blink back my tears.

'They're gorgeous,' Colette said, coming over. 'Can we put them in our dressing room?'

'Of course,' I said, and we began to hunt around for a vase. In the end we found an old pint glass and filled it up with water.

'Uh-oh, looks like we need another one,' Colette said as Fred, the stage doorkeeper, came down with another bunch of flowers – pink carnations this time – and presented them to me.

'They're for me as well!' I gasped.

Fred smiled. 'Looks like you're popular.'

To Sophie, I read. *We'll be cheering you on. Love from Ally, Harriet and Eve.* I smiled. I had the best family and friends in the world!

Just then the tannoy chirped and Lauren's voice came crackling out, sounding like an announcer at an airport. 'Ladies and gentlemen, this is your half hour call. Half an hour please!'

Half an hour. Excitement whooshed through me. This time it was for real!

The TV monitor beside the tannoy flickered and came on. The picture on the screen showed the stage and through the speakers we could hear the sound of people beginning to arrive into the auditorium.

'We should get dressed,' Colette said quickly. 'Come on!'

The half hour flew by and almost before I knew it, Lauren was calling for us to go up to the stage. We hurried up the dark stairs. From the auditorium came the sound of people talking, sweet papers rustling and the orchestra warming up. A trumpet tooted and then a flute trilled. In the wings, at the side of the stage, the stage crew were waiting. It was really dark and, standing with the others, my heart was pounding so fast it felt as if it was going to jump out of my chest.

'Have you heard the news?' Mark said, coming up to Colette and me. 'There're three journalists from national newspapers in tonight.'

I *so* didn't need to know that.

'Really?' Colette gasped.

'And at least two casting agents.'

'Ssh!' Velda hissed. 'Go on into your starting position.'

Mark hurried away to the other side of stage.

'Break a leg!' Colette whispered to me as there was a sudden hush and then the orchestra burst into the overture.

'You too,' I squeaked like a strangled mouse. Colette had told me you never said good luck in a theatre, instead you tell someone to break a leg. It's something weird to do with not tempting fate.

We fell silent. Every second seemed to take an hour.

I had to keep reminding myself to breathe. Every line from the play seemed to have disappeared from my head. I couldn't do this. I really couldn't.

The music changed. The curtains opened and bam! The show started with the first dance. I watched, entranced, as the dancers on stage performed perfectly. And then suddenly, 'Sophie, you're on!' Velda hissed.

Almost before I knew it, I was running on to the stage and into a blaze of light.

That afternoon, I'd thought that things couldn't get any better than the dress rehearsal. OK, how wrong could I be? Performing in front of a packed auditorium was a totally different experience. It was one hundred and fifty per cent – sorry, Harriet – fantastic!

As the curtain fell on the final song the audience erupted with claps and cheers. I stood on stage absolutely stunned. It was over. We'd done it. I hadn't messed up!

'Sophie! Come on!'

Colette grabbed my hand and dragged me into line just as the curtain was sweeping up. The lights hit me and so did the noise. I'd never heard so much clapping.

We all bowed. As we straightened up, I caught sight of Ally and Harriet three rows back. They were standing up cheering. But it wasn't just them. There was Eve, and Mum, Dad, Jess and Tom. And Mr Chase and Emily, Mr and Mrs Swannick and Ally's twin brothers, our next-door neighbours, people from my class in school. In fact, almost everyone I knew seemed to be there and they were all clapping as if they were never going to stop.

In that instant I knew that all the stress and the tension of the rehearsals had been worth it. Standing

on the stage and seeing my friends and family looking so proud of me was one of the best moments of
my life.

One of the best. The other was when I looked at
Ally and Harriet and all my family, and realized
that even if I'd messed up they would still have been
clapping and cheering me. It didn't matter to them
how famous I was or how perfectly I acted. They were
clapping because I was me.

Happiness exploded through my brain and as we
took a final bow and the noise rose to a crescendo, I
wondered what was going to happen next in my life.
There was the rest of the play to do and then what?
A film? A TV show? I didn't know, and as the curtain
began to fall I suddenly realized I didn't care. Things
would happen, life would change, but I knew that
whatever came along my friends and family would be
there for me.

My face split into a wide grin. Now that really *was*
the best feeling of all!

★

Everyone's got different taste . . .

I like stories that make me laugh

Animal stories are definitely my favourite

I'd say fantasy is the best

I like a bit of romance

It's got to be adventure for me

I really love poetry

I like a good mystery

Whatever you're into, we've got it covered . . .

www.puffin.co.uk

hotnews@puffin

Hot off the press!
You'll find all the latest exclusive Puffin news here

Where's it happening?
Check out our author tours and events programme

Bestsellers
What's hot and what's not? Find out in our charts

E-mail updates
Sign up to receive all the latest news
straight to your e-mail box

Links to the coolest sites
Get connected to all the best author web sites

Book of the Month
Check out our recommended reads

www.puffin.co.uk